Trying to Breathe

Under Water

DARBY WEST

ISBN: 978-097902003-2

For

Catherine Elaine McCabe

ACKNOWLEDGMENTS

I would like to acknowledge Orita McCorkle and Allison Griffin, two ladies who helped me set boundaries when I was finally ready.

1

"BENITA, DON'T WAKE YOUR brother and sister," my father said from the front seat. I had made sure not to make any sounds; yet, he was able to hear me. He had to have eyes behind his head! I sat back, leaned my head against the car door, and tried to go to sleep like my brother lying beside me snoring loudly. For a six-year-old kid, Jimmy sure snored loud. I knew without looking at him that his mouth was opened, spit accumulating in the corner, oozing down the side, and gathering in the crook of his arm.

I didn't want to move to Swan Quarter, North Carolina. I wanted to stay in New York in our old apartment in Queens with all of my old friends and my old school! I knew my classmates would return on Monday and wonder what had happened to me.

This was the third time my dad had loaded us all in the car, stuffed the trunk with our luggage, and taken us to someone's house. I was sick of it! I didn't know why he didn't think he could take care of us. He certainly could do a better job than the people he had left us with so far.

"I know you're not sleeping, so why don't you climb up here with me? Help me drive this Caddy," he said.

I took my pillow and climbed up front to sit beside my dad. Because no one had sat in the seat, the leather was cold to my skin. "Can't sleep?"
"Daddy, why do we have to go to live in Swan Quarter? We don't even know these people," I said softly. He patted my hand.

"Come over here beside your daddy." I laid my head on his lap and waited for him to answer my question. "I've done my best, and my best isn't working, baby girl. Your daddy needs help. Mama and Daddy will take good care of y'all.   Aside from the mosquitoes and snakes, it isn't so bad down here." He chuckled. I raised my head, but Daddy patted it back down.

"Just joking with you, sweetie." He sighed loudly and patted my shoulder. "It's all going to work out this time. You'll see."

I closed my eyes and fell asleep. I didn't have any more energy to fight this battle. We were going to have to get used to being down south while our daddy was up in New York. I was angry with my mother for dying six months ago from breast cancer and leaving us like this!

"Wake up! I got us some biscuits and juice," Daddy said. I sat up and rubbed my eyes. It was getting light out now. We were parked in front of a gray, rundown looking house. A sign on the front window said, "Clara's Home Cooking." Daddy held a bag with several sausage and cheese biscuits. The grease had leaked through the wax paper. I took one of the biscuits and began hungrily eating it. My brother, Jimmie, was leaning over the seat and vying for space with my sister, Trina.

"Y'all sit back and eat. We've got to get back on the road before the town wakes up," Daddy said. We were in Norfolk, Virginia; it was not safe for black people to travel in a brand-new car with out-of-state tags in the daytime in 1965. We had to hurry and get out of there. In about three hours, Daddy said we would be at his parent's house. We didn't have this problem in New York; it made me hate where we were going even more.

There was a strange smell in the air. I related it to the hatred in this backward town. It smelled like rotten eggs. It was actually the sulfur in the water I was smelling. But at that time, that is what the smell meant to me – hatred for black people.

2

WE FINALLY PULLED INTO the driveway of his parent's house. I looked around and forced back the tears. Daddy had driven the car around to the backyard. There was a fenced-in pen with several large pigs, wallowing around in the muck. Four brown and white chickens were picking on the ground near a small whitewashed chicken coup. While I was watching in horror, a brown and black rooster strutted out of the coup. There were large oak trees all over the yard; one had a tire and rope hanging from it. Before I could regroup from the shock of that, the back door opened, and a large black cat ran out.

Our grandmother appeared in the doorway, smiling, and clapping her hands. She wasn't much taller than I was, round and her brown face was beaming happily. She wore a scarf on her head, but her long gray braids hung down resting on her large breasts. Though I thought of her as an old woman, her skin was smooth and free of wrinkles, except for the ones at the corner of her eyes when she smiled.

She came down the steps, grinning and wiping tears from her eyes on the towel she held. Daddy hugged her tightly and squealed, "Mommy!"

We stayed in the car until he opened the door to let us out. Jimmy and Trina happily leaped out of the backseat; they were tired of being stuck in a car for what seemed like forever. I, on the other hand, hesitantly got out of the vehicle. Grandma pulled Jimmie into her arms and hugged him. After she released him, she picked up Trina and kissed her fat cheeks.

"I'm going to just eat you up!" Grandma said. Then she looked at me. She held out her arms, waiting for me to enter them. I glanced at Daddy, who gave me "the look." I went to her and hugged her just as tightly as she hugged me. The way she hugged me was assurance she was going to take good care of us. I pressed my face against her ample bosom. She smelled like cinnamon and vanilla with a hint of fried chicken and a big whiff of sweaty boobs.

Daddy took us to his old bedroom and showed us around. There were faded curtains at the window and a beautiful quilt on the bed. He then took us to the room that used to be his sister, Alice's room.

"This is where you all are going to be sleeping. Let me show you where the washroom is," he said. We followed him back down the hallway, through the living room, and out the back door. He walked up to a weird-looking contraption and began pumping the handle. Water came out, and the smell of rotten eggs hit my nose again. "This is the washroom." He motioned toward the contraption.

"What is that?" I asked.

"This is called a pump! Water comes out, and you wash with it. C'mon, girl. Put your hand out," he said. I held out my hands, and he began pumping again. Lukewarm water flowed out of the pump while he stood there laughing, trying to cheer me up.

Then I followed him further into the backyard, where a little brightly painted building was. He opened the door and motioned for me to take a look.

"This is the toilet!" he said grinning. I heard the words leave his lips, but they had not registered. I peered into the little room. There was a wooden board across what looked like a bench, and two cut out circles. There were a couple of rolls of toilet paper and some type of magazine papers on the floor. I stepped inside and Daddy pulled a string that hung from the ceiling, turning on the overhead light bulb. The smell of poop and pee hit my nose and I couldn't back out of there fast enough.

"This is where you go when you want to use the toilet!" he said. I thought he was joking, but the smell let me know he was truly telling the truth!

Four days later, when Daddy was ready to get back into the Caddy and go back to New York, it hit me that he was leaving us and going back home alone. This was going to be our new home. I might as well get used to it!

School had just gotten out a couple of weeks before we got there. Grandma said that most of the children had to help their parents in the fields, which is why school got out early. However, Grandma still got me up early. The first couple of days, I had to force my nine-year-old body out of bed. I was ready to sit on the floor and watch cartoons, but she had other plans for me.

Since I was the oldest, I was going to learn how to feed the pigs, chickens, and bring water into the house in galvanized buckets. I was also responsible for emptying the "nightjar" into the outhouse located back in the furthest part of the yard. When Grandma explained to me what she was talking about, I thought I would throw up. "Are you saying we have to pee and poop in a bucket, and then someone has to take it to that little house and throw it in the hole?" I asked, hoping I had misunderstood her.

"You almost got it right, except that part about it being someone that has to take it out. You are that someone!" she said grinning.

The next morning, I was carrying two buckets with pee and poop in them to the little house. The first time I went in there, the spider webs alone scared the crap out of me. I dropped both buckets, peed on myself, and ran away screaming, trying to pull the webs from my hair. A week later, just like I had done at every other person's house we had stayed with, I was used to it. I woke up when Grandma woke up. She heated water in a large kettle for us to wash up in. We got dressed, and I made up all the beds while she checked behind me to make sure I had done an excellent job.

While she prepared breakfast, my brother and I mixed up corn pellets in water, and I fed them to the nasty hogs. We also fed the chickens. Since I was too big to go into the chicken coup, Jimmie went in to gather the freshly laid eggs. Each morning, the rooster ran him out! He would run to the house, screaming, but tightly holding onto the basket, so he didn't break any eggs. And I emptied two buckets of pee and poop into the hole in the little house.

Our grandfather worked in the tobacco field, driving a tractor. He always looked worn out when he got home in the evening. He would take a quick bath in the basin we all used and put on some old sweatpants and a t-shirt. Dinner was made by the time he joined us.

One day, Grandpa told Jimmie he had a special gift for him. He reached into his pocket and removed a large bright green worm! Jimmie was very impressed with that nasty, fat worm. He was going to make it his pet. Jimmie took a string, tied it around the worm, and let it walk around on the floor. Then one day, Grandma accidentally stepped on it and killed it. Well, she said it was an accident.

After a couple of weeks there, I knew the nightly menu. On Sundays, Grandma cooked a big dinner consisting of fried chicken (not one she raised), baked ham, collard greens, string beans, fried cabbage, candied yams, macaroni and cheese, and we always had rice with each meal. Whatever we ate on Sundays, we had for leftovers on Monday. Tuesdays were pinto beans, rice, and cornbread. Whatever meat she used for cooking the pinto beans in was the only meat we ate. On Wednesdays, we had string beans with some kind of meat cooked in them, little red potatoes she got out of her garden, rice, and cornbread. Thursdays, we had salmon cakes, rice, and squash with onions and cornbread. Fridays, just like Catholics, we always had fish. It was usually fried, rice, and corn on the cob from the garden. She also served sliced tomatoes with onions, salt, and pepper. Saturdays, we had more fish, or if Granddaddy's nephew caught any, we had shrimp and steamed crabs. No matter what we ate, we had rice, homemade buttermilk biscuits, and cornbread. I learned to cook just like my grandmother in the summer of 1965.

Grandma also canned fruits and vegetables she grew in her garden. Early mornings, before the dew dried, she would pick collard greens, tomatoes, cucumbers, cabbage, corn, string beans, white potatoes, carrots, and peas. We would all help her pick apples, pears, and figs. Trina was only two, so she picked up the fruit that had fallen off the trees. Grandma had a grapevine, but she was the only one that picked the grapes because she said sometimes snakes would be in the grapevines. She cleaned and put fish and other seafood in the freezer to eat during the winter. I hoped I wasn't going to be there then. See, I secretly prayed that God would find a way to get me back to New York. I knew my prayers would be answered because that was what I had been taught all my life.

3

"GRANDMA, THERE'S NO WHITE people here?" I asked her one day while we were hanging clothes on the line.

"Of course, there are white folks here! White folks are everywhere," she said, laughing. I had been there for almost two months, and I had not seen one white person. "Why, do you want to see one?"

"There isn't any particular reason; I just thought it strange that I hadn't seen any yet."

That changed the day Grandma asked me to walk with her down to Mrs. Gladys' house to see her sick friend. She made a big pot of chicken feet with rice to take to her. I stood beside the stove as Grandma put the chicken feet and rice into a large bowl.

"Is she really going to eat chicken feet?" I asked.

"They're good for you. What you talking' bout?" she replied, laughing. I was going to have to take her word on that one.

As we walked down the road, we had to move each time a car came along. The grass was high, and I was scared of stepping on a snake.

"The next time you see a stick, pick it up and tap the grass just in case," Grandma said.

"Suppose the stick is really a snake?"

"You worry too much." She picked up a stick and led the way.

As we neared a large white house in the distance, Grandma crossed over to the other side of the road. I followed her, wondering why we had done that. I was about to ask her, but it appeared as if her whole face had changed. Her eyes were no longer the bright, cheery, smiling eyes I was used to. She stared straight ahead; the corners of her mouth turned up. Something awful had just happened, and I had no idea what it could have been. It could even be felt in the air. I walked along, keeping quiet. I eyed the large white house, wondering who lived there and if it had anything to do with the way Grandma changed. I saw a white woman sitting on the porch, and a little girl and boy playing in a small plastic pool.

After we passed the house, the Grandma I knew and loved returned. She said something and smiled. I couldn't hear her because I had fallen behind. I caught up with her and saw she was smiling again; her eyes were warm and friendly.

"Who lives in that house back there?" I asked.
"Just a family. A white family," she added. While she was laughing and talking again, I wondered why she had changed just because we had walked past a white family's house. I reached for her hand; she

looked down at me. Grandma must have read my expression; she kissed my hand and began humming. I couldn't read the expression on her face. I wasn't sure if it was shame or anger. I wanted to let her know that whatever happened, it was okay. I kissed her hand in return.

When we got to her friend's house, she was sitting on the porch, waiting for us. She and Grandma hugged. The friend led us into the house, out of the hot sun.

"Is this pretty little girl your grandbaby, Gert? She's as cute as a bug," she said, smiling. A *bug?* Did she think that was a compliment? I didn't want to be cute as a bug! What came to my mind was that big brown water bug under the washing machine the other day. When I stepped on it, the crunch was so loud I jumped back, surprised.

"She's going to be tall as me if she keeps eating like

she does. Gladys, this is Benita. Say Hi, Benita," Grandma said. Ms. Gladys opened her arms and pulled me to her. She was a frail woman. I felt the bones along her back when she hugged me.

Grandma fixed the chicken feet and rice in a bowl, buttered a couple of her buttermilk biscuits, and placed them on a tray to take to Ms. Gladys. While she ate her dinner, Grandma swept her kitchen and washed the few dishes in the sink. I helped by drying them off and putting them back in the cupboard. Her water buckets were empty, so Grandma told me to get them and go outside and get some water from the pump. When I returned, we stayed a few more minutes and then went home.

Just like before, as we passed the large white house, Grandma got quiet and walked along, holding my hand, her head high, but with the same expression on her face. I didn't know how to bring it up, so I let it go. I hated to see my grandmother look this way. I turned my head and looked away.

Aside from that puzzling experience, I learned a lesson that has remained with me to this day: We have an obligation to each other to help when we can, even if it is a sacrifice to us. I have to help the less fortunate, sick, and elderly. That's just the way it is!

I tried to block out whatever bad thing happened and concentrate on the positive things that had happened. Try as I might, I could not get it out of my head. While we were washing the dinner dishes, I decided to bring it up.

"Grandma, do you know the people that live in that big white house?" I asked.

A shadow seemed to appear around her face. She washed two plates before she answered. "Yes, I know them. Why?"

"Did they do something to you?" I asked, pushing

further.

"The husband there takes care of my momma's land. He's a farmer," she said, still not answering my question.

"He's a nice man?"

"He's a lot of things, but the word nice will never mean nothing to him."

She picked up the basin of dirty dishwater and went out the back door, letting the screen swing shut loudly. I went behind her. I knew she would pour the water into the pigpen. Then she would go to the pump and rinse out the dishpan.

"Where does this water come from?"

"From the ground. Your granddaddy had a man dig a hole until he hit the water. It's like a well," she explained, not looking at me.

"I love you, Grandma."

She turned suddenly to look at me. Grandma put the dishpan on top of the pump and instructed me to follow her around to the front of the house.

She sat on the step and patted the space beside her.

"Things down here are different from up in New York. Down here, white folks think they better than everybody else. They are no different though'; meaner, maybe. But they believe that they better. All that land that house is on used to belong to my momma and poppa. It belonged to their poppas, too. From down there where they live, all the way up to that oak tree right there is our land. You can't see it from here, but there is a stake near that tree. They took that land, knowing we didn't have the money to fight to get it back. My daddy cursed that land. It looks like he might be thriving now, but his day will come. Watch, see don't it!"

I hugged her tightly, relieved that the look I saw on her face wasn't one of fear, but defiance! I loved my grandma more that day.

"Let's go on inside and rest," she said. That was the last time I ever heard her say those words to me again. I stood up and reached for her hand to help pull her up.

"I love you, Grandma." She kissed me on the cheek and patted my face. Even though she had never said it, I knew she loved me.

4

SCHOOL DIDN'T START THAT year in that little town. I heard the grown-ups talking, but they always ran me from the room, so I never knew exactly what was going on.

"Benita, get up honey. Get Jimmy and Trina up too. All of you, get dressed for church," she said.
Church? It wasn't even a Sunday! My ears had to be playing a trick on me.

"Where are we going again?" I asked to be sure.
"We're going to church," was all she said. We didn't have to walk past the big white house. We went another way. The roads were so flat I could look down the road at least a mile. My little sister started complaining about being tired; Grandma and I took turns picking her up and carrying her. Finally, we

arrived at the street where the church was. Up ahead, I saw a crowd of people gathered. I had not seen that many people since moving from New York.

"Who are all of those people, Grandma?" I asked.
"It looks like every black person in Hyde County is here," she said, smiling. There was a twinkle in her eyes, and I was proud. I put my sister down on the ground and reached for Grandma's hand. She looked at me, smiling, and hugged me.

I felt so good that day; I just wanted to run and hug all of these black people who had come out to fight for their civil rights. We were going to be just like the folks we saw on television protesting in Birmingham, Montgomery, and Atlanta. I was so excited!

That first day of protests was exciting. We walked in twos all the way downtown, singing and clapping our hands. As we passed the large homes, where white people lived, I saw them sitting on their porches, watching us. I looked toward Grandma to see she was still smiling, happy, and eyes were beaming. Not all of the homes were large houses, some of them were trailers or rundown shacks, and the people who lived there looked dirty, hungry, and mean. I even saw some of the men holding rifles. But we kept marching, singing, and clapping.

When we got downtown, the leader, Mr. Golden Frinks, gave a speech. I wanted to know what and why we were protesting. I listened intently, holding my sister's hand tightly so that she didn't get lost in the crowd.

When it became apparent to me what the purpose of this protest was, I was puzzled. What was going on was that the all-white county commissioners wanted to destroy one of the black schools and bus all the black children to one remaining school. It was already overcrowded and lacked funding for repairs;

yet, the white children were being taught in a beautiful new school.

You mean to tell me that black children and white children went to different schools? They didn't go to the same schools? Why? What was that about?

In my Queens, New York neighborhood, there were people from all over the place living there. An Italian family lived next door. A Puerto Rican family lived across the street, and upstairs from us, lived a West Indian family. We all went to the same school. I thought it was like that all over the place. But down here, it was different. I felt things needed to change; I looked forward to the next days' protests.

Ms. Carrie, who lived across the road, told Grandma she would watch Jimmie and Trina. We didn't have to make them walk to the church each day. That was a relief! Now I had a chance to mingle with young people my age, and Grandma was free to be with her friends. Each day that we marched downtown, a news reporter joined us. She wandered through the crowds, interviewing teenagers, and getting their opinion about things going on.

One day, I was sitting on the steps of the church, just thinking about things. I had seen some of the people whose trailers we passed. Their children were playing outside with the dogs, chickens, or goats. Their clothes were dirty and worn out. The windows were broken out of their trailers, and they looked destitute; yet, they believed that even in their wretched conditions, they were better than even the most educated black person. I just couldn't understand that.

"What are you thinking about?" the reporter asked. The cameraman came up beside her, his camera trained on me. I knew her name was Robin because I had heard her being called before. I looked up, surprised by her presence. "What are you thinking about? You looked deep in thought," she said.

Did she really want to hear what I had to say? I was just a ten-year-old girl from New York who found myself in this town only because my mother had died. I could think of at least one other place I would rather be.

"I was thinking about this family I saw earlier today. They lived in one of those trailers we have to pass to get downtown," I replied. She sat next to me on the step.

"Why did you think about them?" she asked, holding out her tape recorder in front of me.

"They are poor; really poor. Yet, when we pass their house, the kids throw things at us. They think they are better than us. It's weird."

"Where are you from? I hear a Northern accent."

"I'm from Queens, New York."

"I bet the school you went to up there was integrated, huh?"

"It was, that's why this whole thing is sad to me."

As I said it, tears rolled down my face and onto my knees. I wiped them away and put my head down. Robin patted my head as if I were a puppy and walked away.

When we got home that evening, Granddaddy told me that he saw me on the news. It touched him deeply. The next morning, and every morning of the protests, he gave Grandma and me a ride to the church before he went to work in the fields.

I hoped that Daddy saw me on the news and saw what being in this racist town was doing to me, and would come and get me, Jimmy, and Trina. He didn't see me though, and I doubted that Grandma told him how hard this was affecting me.

When I was told that Mommy was sick, I thought it was just a cold, chickenpox, or something simple like that. Even when she had to stop working, I didn't

know the seriousness of her illness. At first, I would come home from school and she would be in the kitchen, still in her pajamas, but trying to make us dinner. Trina was only about a year old then. She would be laying in her playpen sleeping while Mommy tried to cook. In between stirring the pots, she would
sit down like she was so very tired. Soon she was telling me to fix a hot dog for me and my siblings, she didn't feel good.

I didn't realize how serious this must be until one day I came home and she was in the bathroom looking at herself in the mirror. Before she had gotten sick she wore her hair in a big Afro. She kept it braided at night and never let it loose. But, this day it was loose and she was picking it. All around her feet were clumps of her hair. I thought she had cut it, but as she picked it, it was just coming out and falling slowly to the floor. She was crying and picking her hair.

I couldn't even say anything! I went to the living room and sat down on the sofa, hugging a pillow and crying. I couldn't tell anyone why I was crying, but it hurt me, that my mother was hurting. She was in and out of the hospital, sometimes coming home wearing a mask, and we couldn't come near her because we 'could get her sicker'.

5

I DIDN'T KNOW HOW THIS protest was going to end, or what the outcome would be. Would it just be a year? It had only been four months, and I was tired. I wanted to be in school!

"Are you okay?" a voice asked. I raised my head to see a very handsome teenage boy sitting next to me. I had seen him before, nearly every day actually, but I didn't know his name.

I wiped my eyes and mumbled, "I'm okay."

He gently rubbed my back and said, "Everything is going to be okay. Just hang in there."

"I just want to go back to New York! I don't want to stay here no more!"

"We're making a change here. Once it's made you'll feel better that you at least helped."

As he talked, he looked right into my eyes. He walked away, and for the next few months, I dreamed about him every night! His name was Henry, and he was gorgeous!

So far, all of the protests were peaceful. But one morning when I got up, I had a feeling in the pit of my stomach that something horrible was going to happen. Grandma wasn't going to the church with me, but she let me go with two of the teenagers, Kevin and Cheryl, from down the road who were walking to the church. When we got to the church, we did what we always did, which was organized into twos, and start marching downtown.

We sang the same songs we always sang; we passed the same houses we had always passed. I tried to shake that feeling, but it wasn't going anywhere. Once we got downtown, all hell broke loose! Some teenagers were standing on the steps of the courthouse, and Mr. Frink's son, Allen, was speaking.

His tone was different than Mr. Frink's. Allen was more Malcolm X than Dr. King.

Suddenly, the teenagers were going through the doors of the courthouse, running. They were running all over the place. I got lost in the crowd, and Grandma had stressed that I should not leave Cheryl's side. I had to find her. I started running, too, trying to search for her or her brother. Pillows of smoke were everywhere; the deputies had thrown tear gas into the crowd.

My eyes were burning, and the kids were screaming. I saw several white deputies hitting us with their police sticks. I ran from the crowd and the chaos and ended up near the jail. A group of teenagers was being pushed and forced toward the jail. I tried to get out of the crowd, but it was too late. I was forced into a jail cell with at least fifty teenagers.

One of them saw me in their midst and yelled for the

jailer to let me out, "She's a kid!" Then he was joined by others. My eyes were burning from the tear gas, and I was crying because I knew my Grandma was going to be worried about me. I saw the camera crews from the news, and if she saw this on TV, she was going to panic. I just held onto the bars and cried my heart out.

Finally, I was let out of jail. I lived three miles from downtown. I couldn't find Cheryl or her brother. It was dark outside now. I had nowhere to go. There were parents outside picking up their children, but there was no one for me. What was I going to do? I didn't dare attempt to walk home in the dark alone. I was afraid of that road in the daytime.

Besides, I thought about all of those mean white people just waiting for the opportunity to use those rifles they were trying to intimidate us with. I didn't know what to do. If I could get to a phone, I could have called home, and Grandpa would have come for me, but I didn't even see a payphone anywhere. I didn't recognize any of the people there to ask them to take me home.

I started crying and went to sit down on the steps of the courthouse. I was sitting there, crying, and contemplating what would happen to me if I didn't get home. Then I heard Cheryl calling my name. I looked up, thankful that she was there. "C'mon, let's go. My daddy is here to get us," she said. I hugged her tightly and was afraid to let her go.

I cried all the way home. I just wanted to go back to New York. I begged my grandma to let me call my daddy that night. "Please, come get me, Daddy, please," I begged.

"All right, I'll come to get you this weekend," he promised. Grandma also thought it was a good idea. She would keep my siblings, but I would go back to live with daddy.

6

DADDY CAME DOWN EARLY Saturday morning. I was so glad to see him! On Saturday night, after it got dark, we hit the road heading back to New York. I lay down in the back seat and fell fast asleep. I hoped that when I woke up, I would be back in Queens, and I could go back to school with decent people who were respectful of others.

I had no idea what the southern school system would be like once this protest was over, and the schools were integrated. I knew I didn't want to be around to find out. Perhaps by the time Jimmie and Trina were old enough to go to school, the chaos would be settled, and they would be okay.

We arrived back in New York late in the morning. I was so glad to see my old neighborhood; I kissed the ground. I kissed the steps to our apartment. I kissed the door. I kissed the rug in our living room.

"Call your grandma and let her know we made it home, and get up off that floor!" Daddy said, laughing. It was almost 10:30.

Grandma was up, washing the breakfast dishes, or feeding the animals. I told her we had gotten home safely, and after I took a nap, I would call her back. "I love you, Grandma."
"Y'all take care," she replied.

I ate a big bowl of Lucky Charms cereal, and then another and another. Grandma didn't buy cold cereal; well, she purchased those nasty hunks of shredded wheat, but that is where she drew the line. After I was stuffed, I lay down in the living room and turned on the TV. I hadn't seen a cartoon in the entire nine months I had been down south.

While Daddy slept peacefully in the bedroom, I enjoyed all of the things I had been deprived of while visiting the south. I got a slice of cheese pizza from Mr. Tony's and lemon ice. Later, I ate a Knish and a Jamaican meat patty. For dinner, I had Chinese food. I was so glad to be home! I missed all my neighborhood restaurants.

While Daddy slept, I took some money from his wallet and got the house keys so I could get some candy from Mr. Bruce's candy store. I filled a bag with a Sugar Daddy, several Mary Janes, Now and Laters, Raisinettes, Jawbreakers, Bazookas, and Pumpkin Seeds. Daddy was still sleeping when I got home. It was quiet and peaceful; as a result, I also fell asleep.

It wasn't one of those peaceful nights of sleep. No! I tossed and turned, and I heard myself talking and laughing in my sleep. I was home, but it took me nearly a week to calm down at night and sleep peacefully!

On Monday, Daddy took me to school to get enrolled. Because I had been out for six months of the school year, I had to take a test to see if I could join my class in the fifth grade, or be sent back to fourth. I sat in the library, facing the librarian, completing the test. It was easy! I knew I had this in the bag. I joined my classmates in the fifth grade.

Daddy made arrangements for my after-school care. I was to go to Ms. Rose's house after school. She lived four blocks from our house. I wouldn't have to walk down there by myself because several of my classmates lived down that way.

Ms. Rose had several adult children who no longer lived at home, but she had two kids still there. Jerry and Mary were their names. Mary was sixteen; Jerry was nineteen. Though he should have been working, he wasn't. Jerry stayed home all day, playing records, smoking weed, and harassing Mary and her friends.

Even though Daddy was paying Ms. Rose to watch me, I was often left with Mary while Ms. Rose did whatever she was doing outside of the house. My father never knew this because I didn't tell him.

When I got to Ms. Rose's house, she made me sit at the table in the kitchen and do my homework while she cooked dinner for her family. Even when she was not there, I sat at the kitchen table until I was finished with my homework. Then I went to Mary's room and watched TV.

One day, I was seated in the beanbag chair in Mary's room while she looked through a magazine. When her phone rang, she told someone she would be right over. "You can stay up here. I have to go to my friend's house around the corner and get something. I'll be back in about an hour," she said. Mary put on her shoes and left.

Not long after she left, Jerry came upstairs and asked, "Where's Mary?"

"She went to her friend's house, but she will be back in an hour," I replied. He came in and sat down in the chair beside the TV.

"Whatcha watching?" he asked, putting his hands in front of the TV to block my view.

"Stop it, Jerry!" I shouted. He came over, picked me up, and threw me on the bed.

"Get out of my room!" Mary yelled. It startled Jerry, and he backed away from me. I got up and smoothed down my skirt. As he walked past her, she punched him in the back.

"Freak!" she shouted. I heard him laughing as he walked down the hallway. "Did he try to touch you?"

"No, he was just messing with me," I replied.

"Stay away from him; he's crazy!" she warned.

7

DADDY AND I HAD GONE to Brooklyn to shop for shoes at Alexander's Department Store. After he purchased my shoes, we stopped at a fish n' chips place on Nostrand Avenue and got enough fried fish to last for dinner on Sunday. When we were on our way home, he said, "I have a date tonight."

"Who do you have a date with?" I didn't even know he was seeing anyone.

"I just met this beautiful lady that lives around the corner, and she invited me over to a little get-together," he said, smiling.

What's her name?"

"Her name is Leila," he said, still smiling.

I felt a little jealous but mostly worried. Would she

want to move in with us and have me sent to live with someone else, like that crazy Liz lady that tried to take over our lives? She was the reason why we had been packed up and sent away the second time. Daddy found us another place to live. I sank into the seat and stared out of the window, not saying anything.

While we were eating dinner, Daddy said, "You're going to be spending the night with Ms. Rose."

Yeah! That's what he thought! I was going to be looked after by Mary. I packed an overnight bag, got my stocking cap, and toothbrush out of the bathroom.
"I'm ready," I shouted.

Daddy had been in his bedroom for at least an hour, getting dressed to go to this raggedy get-together. When he finally stepped out of the room, he had shaved his beard off, cut his hair, and smelled like he had taken a dip in the Old Spice. He was wearing a black turtleneck, black slacks, and a bright red jacket. I had to smile!

"You look so handsome, Daddy."
"I know that!" he teased and spun around like the Temptations.

When we got to Ms. Rose's house, she was there, which was usually the case. We stood in the doorway, waving bye to Daddy as he drove off in his Caddy. She reached out for her coat and slipped her feet into her heels.

"Y'all don't keep this child up all night long. I'll see you in the morning," she said.

I followed Mary into the kitchen and sat down at the table while she made us some Jiffy popcorn and root beer floats. I carried the pan of popcorn, and she had the drinks. As we passed Jerry's bedroom, he whistled like those nasty men do when they see a pretty woman in the street. I knew he wasn't whistling at me, and he had to be sick if he was whistling at this own sister.

"Freak!" Mary shouted.

She locked her bedroom door, and I sat down on the bed while she found something for us to watch on the TV.

"I want you to be careful around Jerry. He's crazy," she said.

"Why do you keep telling me that? What does he do?" I asked.

"He's nasty. He likes to feel up on girls. If he ever touches you, I want you to tell me, okay?" I promised that I would.

Mary and I went to the movies one Saturday afternoon to see Shaft. Two of her teenage friends came along. We were not old enough to see this "R" rated movie, but no one cared in the hood. I spent most of the movie with my face with Mary's hair covering my face.

After the movie, we stopped for pizza. I liked being around them. They talked about boys, clothes, Soul Train, and did I mention boys? I listened, eating it all up. On the way home, after her friends got to their houses, Mary and I walked down the block, holding hands. Just as we turned the corner, we met Jerry. He had gone to pick up the Chinese food their mom had ordered. He was grinning at Mary, but she hawked and spat a loogie on the ground near him. He laughed loudly and kept walking behind us.

When we got to the house, I followed Mary to her room and hung up my coat. "Stay in here. I'll be right back," she said.

I took off my sneakers and climbed up on the top bunk. No sooner than she had left out of the room,

Jerry came in. He put his finger to his lips, motioning for me to be quiet. He came to the bunk bed and whispered, "Give me some sugar."

I moved toward the wall. He reached for my foot and dragged me to the edge of the bed. I tried to pull away from his grasp, but he grabbed my head and pulled me to him. His lips were cold and tasted like grape soda. I was saying, "No! Stop!" but his tongue was in my mouth. He pulled away and walked out quickly. I slid back toward the wall and wiped my mouth vigorously with the sheet.

When Mary came back, I told her what had happened. "Ma! Jerry's messing with Bennie! I'm gonna bust his ass!" she shouted.

Mary ran down the hallway toward Jerry's bedroom. "Open this door! You nasty bastard!" she screamed and banged on the door.

The bedroom door opened, and Ms. Rose was

standing there. "What did he do to you?" she asked.

"He kissed me and put his tongue in my mouth," I said, trying to talk through the tears.

I put the pillow over my head to drown out the screaming and the fighting. It sounded like Mary was killing him! I could hear furniture falling, breaking, and Jerry screaming he hadn't done anything, that I was lying. I wanted to go home! I just wanted to be with my daddy! I climbed down the ladder and grabbed my coat and shoes. I ran out of their house and ran all the way home.

My father wasn't home, so I sat on the step, waiting for him. It was cold outside. My neighbor, Mrs. Anderson, heard me crying and let me stay at her house. I was too afraid to tell her what had happened at Ms. Rose's home. I didn't even tell my daddy.

The next weekend, when Daddy dropped me off at Ms. Rose's house, I tried to stay as close to Mary as I could. I even went with her to the bathroom. I didn't see Jerry the entire weekend, and I was glad of that. But I wondered how long I was going to be able to avoid him.

I was only eleven years old. I didn't have real breasts, yet. I had just started getting hair under my arms. Mary's friends would have certainly been a better choice. They were already having sex with boys. I was just a little kid! *I was just a little kid!*

8

I HAD FALLEN ASLEEP ON the bottom bunk. Since I was sleeping, Mary went down the block to her friend Jackie's house for just a few minutes. I woke up to someone tugging at my shorts. It was Jerry. "No, No!" I screamed.

He put his hand over my mouth. "If you scream again, I swear to God, I will kill you," he said, slapping me twice across the face.

I tasted the blood in my mouth. I had to get out of this body! Jerry put one hand around my throat, pulled down my panties with the other, and began thrusting himself into me. With each thrust, I felt myself ripping to accommodate him. I tried to die. I decided to stop breathing and just die. What had I done to make him want to hurt me?

I heard a loud sound, like something breaking. He grunted as if the wind had been knocked out of him, and collapsed on. Something warm was running down my face as he lay on me. Each time he grunted, he tried to say something. I screamed and screamed, then passed out. He had fallen off the bunk bed and was on the floor.

Mary was hitting him with a bat over and over. The awful thud sounds were his bones being crushed. Blood was all over the walls, the dresser, the front of her shirt, her face, and her arms. Blood was all over me, as well. Jerry's lifeless body lay on the floor of her room, a bloody mess I could not even make out his face because she had destroyed it.

I ran into the bathroom and closed the door. I wanted my daddy! I just wanted my daddy! There were clothes racks in the tub, drying Mary's clothes.

I put on one of the dresses draped over the rack and ran from the house. I didn't even have on shoes, but I didn't care. I didn't stop running until I got to Mrs. Anderson's home. I banged on the door and cried for her to answer. She looked at me in horror. "Oh, my God! Who did this to you?" she cried. I probably looked worse than what I felt since I had blood splattered on my face and arms.

She took me to the emergency room, where I was seen immediately by a doctor. My body was lying on that bed, but I was long gone. I was drowning. From up high, I saw the nurses and the doctor taking care of me, stitching, probing, lifting, and touching me. Afterward, I was taken to a room in the children's ward. There was a little girl in the other bed. She was sleeping when I was placed on the bed, and the curtain was closed. I turned to face the window. I wondered how high up we were. If it were high enough, I was ready to throw myself out of the window and end it all.

When I woke up the next morning, Daddy was sitting in the recliner beside my bed, sleeping. The clock on the wall read 12:30. I had been sleeping since the previous night!

He stirred, but I didn't want to face him. I turned away and pretended to be still sleeping. I wondered if Mary was in jail. Was Jerry dead? Why did he do this to me? *Just breathe!*

When I woke up the second time, Daddy was awake. He stood up and pulled me to him, hugging me, begging me to forgive him for leaving me there. "I didn't know, sweetie! I didn't know," he kept saying.

"Where is Mary?" I asked.
"She's home with her mother. She's going to be okay," he said reassuringly.
I wondered how that could be. Mary had killed her brother. She wasn't going to be *okay*!
That afternoon, I was released and went home with

my father. I wanted to get back to what I had been doing, but I never wanted to go to Ms. Rose's house ever again.

9

I GOT DRESSED FOR SCHOOL Monday morning and went outside, just like I usually did and walked with my friends. They laughed and made fun of each other. Even though I wasn't my usual self, no one noticed. At the time, I thought it was a good thing. I didn't have to answer any questions about why I was quiet. I just blended in with all that was going on around me.

Now, instead of going to Ms. Rose's house when Daddy had a date or worked late, I stayed in the apartment. As long as the door was locked, I felt safe.

Mrs. Anderson promised to check in on me, and if I were ever frightened, I could go upstairs to her apartment. I didn't know what good that would have done because my "fright" went everywhere I went. It never showed itself to anyone but me. Once Daddy got dressed, he asked me over and over if I would be okay. "Yes! I am fine. Go out!" I replied. After he left, I locked all three front door locks, and then walked through the entire apartment, making sure the windows were still locked, blinds closed, and curtains tightly pulled together.

I fixed myself a snack consisting of soda, chips and dip, and a dill pickle. I turned off all of the lights, except the one in the bathroom, lay down on the couch, and watched TV until Daddy came home. Every outside noise startled me. I had to get up and make sure all three door locks were still locked, windows bolted, blinds closed, and curtains tightly drawn. I did that at least five times a night. *Breathe!*

I went through the sixth grade, and all the other grades blended into uneventful experiences. I had a few associates I spent time with, but only one I honestly called a friend. Her name was Nadine. She lived in the co-ops by my school in the Bronx. She was the only one willing to ride the subway to Queens to meet me on the weekend. We went to the movies, window shopping, or just walked around in the Village.

Nadine's family was from Trinidad. She reminded me of the people from India. I will never forget the first time I went to her home. She lived on the twelfth floor of their building. Nadine answered the door. I was just about to step inside when a tall figure ran down the hallway and tackled me to the floor, knocking the wind out of me. I screamed and began punching him, kicking, and trying to get him off of me. *Breathe!*

Nadine and her father pulled the man off of me. He was laughing and saying something unintelligible. Her father apologized profusely for what happened.

He took the man and led him away.

"Sorry about that. That's my little brother, Carlton. He's retarded," she explained. I had heard that word used to describe someone foolish or had said something stupid as a cruel joke that kids spoke. I had never actually met anyone who was a special needs person. She shrugged it off and took my hand, leading me inside.

Her mom was in the kitchen, cooking with a big pot boiling away on the stove. She wiped her hands on the towel hanging from her apron. Her smile was warm and inviting; it removed a tiny bit of the fright I felt from the big, burly man who tackled me.

Nadine's father returned to the room and apologized again. "Nadine told you Carlton is retarded? He didn't mean any harm. He forgets his size sometimes, but he is just a big teddy bear. He gets excited around strangers," he said, smiling, probably hoping it would comfort me, but it didn't. It had stirred up memories from when Jerry... I accepted their apology and tried to forget what happened. I knew, at that moment, I would never be able to revisit Nadine. *Breathe!*

When I got home that afternoon, I took a shower, scrubbing my body until it was sore. I dried off and put on my pajamas. Before getting comfortable for the evening, I made sure the door was locked, windows locked, blinds shut, and curtains tightly drawn. I unlocked and locked the door to make sure it was locked. *Breathe!*

Mahogany, the movie, was on that evening. I sat in front of the TV with a bowl of popcorn, chips, dip, and a one-liter bottle of grape soda. And tried as I might, I could not forget how Nadine's brother had run and tackled me to the floor.

"No! No!" I said, sitting up, clutching my chest. *Just relax. Breath. Count. Relax. It's okay. It's over.*

You're home now. Just relax. I tried to repeat to myself all of the things I typically said to calm down. *I was drowning again.*

10

BY THE TIME I WAS SIXTEEN, I was having a tough time. "Daddy, I think I've had panic attacks," I said one morning. We were sitting at the table, eating breakfast.

"Whatcha talking about?" he asked.

"Sometimes, I can't breathe, and my chest hurts. I break out in a sweat. I'm scared, and I want to talk to a doctor. A psychiatrist." I had looked up panic attacks in the encyclopedia.

He sat there, looking at me for a few seconds. My hand was shaking. "You can say something," I said nervously.

"Why don't you get out of the house, spend some

time with people your age. You don't hang out with your friends," he said.

"I go places. I just want to see a psychiatrist. I've never talked to anyone about what happened..." I started to explain.

"You know what! We're not going to talk about going to see no damn shrink! You're gonna get off your butt and hang out with your friends!" he shouted.

He stood up suddenly and took out his wallet. He threw some money on the table; some landed in my food. "Go out and do something! There is nothing wrong with you, except you need to get out of this house!" He had tears in his eyes, but he sounded angry. *Breathe!*

He grabbed his keys and left. I got up and made sure all three door locks were locked. I checked all the windows to make sure they were locked, blinds closed, and curtains are drawn.

I was trying to breathe underwater. My father was saying all I needed to do was get out of the house, mingle with my friends, and all would be well. I screamed; I screamed as loud as I could.

Mrs. Anderson was knocking on the door and calling my name, but I couldn't answer the door. "I'm okay. Just leave me alone. I'm okay!" I yelled at her.
"No, baby! Please, open this door! I want to help you," she begged.

I went to the bathroom and shut the door. I turned on the shower and the sink to drown out her voice.

She finally gave up and returned to her apartment. I came out of the bathroom and checked the door to make sure it was locked. I checked the windows. *Breathe!*

It was a little past ten o'clock when I knocked on Ms. Rose's door. I had dressed in all black, put a baseball cap on, and rushed to her house. I saw Mary in the window. She closed the drapes and came to the door just as I was about to leave.

I hadn't seen her in four years, not since that night. She looked old, haggard beyond her years. "How are you doing?" she asked.
"How are you?" I asked. I wanted to hear her answer first.

She shook her head vigorously and tried to smile. "I'm…I'm okay," she finally said. "I'm not. I just wanted to see if you were okay. Is Jerry dead?" I asked, knowing already that he was.

"Yes, he died that night. Listen, it wasn't your fault. Come on, let's walk." When we got down the steps to the sidewalk, I saw Ms. Rose in the window.

"Jerry raped me when he was fourteen. He was sick, Bennie. My mom kept making excuses for him until he tried to attack her, too. She threatened to kill him if he tried it again. So, he tried me again. I told him the next time I would kill him. He never bothered me after that. But when you started coming over, I saw that look in his eyes again. I knew if he touched you, I was going to kill him. I had told him that, but he didn't listen," she said, smoking a cigarette, her hand trembling.

"Did you go to jail, Mary?" I asked.
She nodded. "I went to a hospital for coo-coo people," she said, laughing nervously.

"I just wanted to make sure you were okay," I said again. I awkwardly hugged her and went back home. I unlocked and locked the door. I checked the windows to make sure they were all locked, blinds closed, and curtains were drawn, and I tried to breathe. *I tried to breathe! Just breathe!*

I checked my father's liquor cabinet to see if he had any clear alcohol. I had heard one of my classmates say that clear alcohol didn't leave a smell on your breath. Daddy had a bottle of Beefeater's and a bottle of Tanqueray. The Tanqueray was in a green bottle and looked expensive. I didn't know what color it was, so I put it back. I poured some of the Beefeater's in a plastic cup and got my usual lineup of snack foods. When I gulped it down, the drink burned my nostrils. I had to gasp for air. Whoa! It was strong!

Within twenty minutes, I was knocked out. I fell asleep, and for once in the five years since Jerry had forced himself into me, I slept all night long. Gin became my new best friend. I took my allowance and purchased my own bottle and hid it behind the sofa. Every day I poured gin into my water bottle and took it to school with me. It was easy to hide my drinking because I rarely talked to anyone.

My father felt that as long as I had food, clothes, money, and a place to live that all was well. He didn't notice I had changed from a happy child to one whose innocence had been stolen at just eleven years old! How was he to see that I walked around frightened all the time? I spent more time locking and unlocking the front door than was necessary. I fought each day to just breathe. He didn't notice my drunken phase because he didn't want to.

11

MRS. SPENCER, MY ENGLISH teacher told us that to get full credit for this report, we had to be on a team. As soon as I heard the word team, my panic levels shot up. I didn't want to be on a team! I raised my hand for the first time since being in high school. "Why can't we do this report alone? I mean, do we have to be on a team?" I asked nervously. *Please, say it's okay to be alone. Please! Please!*

"No, you have to be on a team. I've already set them up. On your way out today, check the notice on the wall by the door. Oh yeah, a team doesn't necessarily mean a bunch of people. In this case, a team is just one other person. Good luck, class!" she said.

I knew she was looking at me when she said it, but I refused to make eye contact with her. I gathered my things and rushed out of the class without looking at the notice. I didn't care who she put me with; I wasn't going to be on a team. I would just take my "F" grade. I didn't care!

I sat outside, eating my bologna sandwich and sipping my gin when this boy came and sat down. "Hey! It looks like we are a team," he said, smiling.

"What are you talking about?" I asked, forgetting the class assignment. "Oh, that," I replied after he refreshed my memory.

"I'm Steven," he said. I knew who he was. Every girl in school knew who he was. He was the star basketball player, football player, tennis player, and the coolest guy in school – or so the girls thought. His skin was brown, smooth, and unblemished. He had thick eyebrows and long lashes. His brown eyes were piercing into me. He crossed his long legs and continued smiling. He had the whitest teeth I had ever seen on a person. I knew who he was, and didn't care. I looked at him again and took a long sip of my gin.

He was eyeing me funny. "Are you okay?"
I took another long swig. "I'm cool," I said. I screwed the lid back on and put the bottle in my backpack.
"I wrote my number down so we can start our assignment today. Did you get a chance to read the suggested topics?" he asked.

When I looked directly at him, I swear I saw six of him. I tried to focus, but I was so high I just saw his mouths moving, and the words were all jumbled. I nodded to everything he said. I silently wished he would get out of my face because I wasn't going to do this assignment with him. He could forget about it! He was holding out his hand with something in it.

I reached for it and threw it in my backpack, never looking at it.

"You take care," he said and walked away.

I went to my final class, where I stared off into space the whole time the teacher talked. No one ever called on me, so I wasn't concerned about them noticing I was drunk.

A few days later, Steven gave me some information he wanted me to research. I looked down at the paper and back at him. "I got your number from your friend, Nadine. I tried to call you to find out what topic you wanted to write about. You never returned my call, so I picked one for us. We're going to talk about the importance of a healthy lunch at school. I have nearly completed the outline and some of the actual essay, but I wanted to give you a chance to offer some input," he said. Steven paused, waiting to see what I had to say. I didn't care what he wrote about.

"Benita, are you okay?" he asked. I looked at him this time, only seeing one of him. He seemed really concerned about me.

"I'm okay."

"I don't think you are." He gave me his number again. "If you ever want to talk, I'm here."

I took the paper he placed on my desk and folded it this time and put it in my pocket. "Thank you."

When I got home, I decided to look at the assignment the teacher wanted us to write. I didn't want to be challenging to work with, but I wished she hadn't put us in teams. I didn't want Steven to get a poor grade because I didn't want to be part of a team. I dialed his number and waited.

"Hello, this is Benita. May I speak to Steven?"

"This is Steven."

"Hi, I finally looked over the assignment. Do you need any help?"

"Well, it is supposed to be a team effort. So, yeah, I think I will need help." He chuckled.

We discussed how far he had come on the assignment. I said, "I will do some research and write down what I find out about nutritious meals and give it to you tomorrow."
"I saw your handwriting, and you write a whole lot better than I do. I think you should write it up."

In the school library, we sat across from each other and added the finishing touches to our assignment. Steven had made a chart and posted pictures of fruit and vegetables on it. At first, it looked juvenile, but he said his dad worked in advertising and could take it to work with him and make it look professional.

Steven and I both received "A" grades. When he hugged me, I was surprised I didn't flinch from his touch. It caught me off guard, but it was a friendly hug.

After the assignment was done, I wondered if we would continue to get to know each other, or would that be the end of us. That afternoon, I was sitting in my usual space, eating my lunch all alone when Steven came over, carrying a takeout container. "Can I join you?" he asked. I motioned for him to sit down.

"Why are you always out here by yourself?"
"I don't have any friends."
"I've seen you with Nadine before, what happened?"
Did I dare tell him that her special-needs brother scared the crap out of me when I went to visit her? No, I couldn't tell him that. "I don't know," I lied.

He was eating his Chinese food with chopsticks, and I was impressed. "Do you live in Brooklyn?" I asked.
"Yeah, in Park Slope. What about you?"
"I live in Queens."
"Would you like to go to the movies on Saturday?"

he asked suddenly.

"Can I call you later? I have to think about it."

"Okay, that's fine," he said.

I agreed to go to the movie with Steven, but I wanted to make sure it was okay with my father. When Steven came to pick me up that evening, Daddy was there to ask him questions to make sure he was on the up and up. I excused myself and went to my bedroom. I had a bottle of Beefeater's Gin in the back of my closet. I unscrewed it and was about to take a swig, then stopped. I wanted to be sober today. I put on some earrings, got my sweater and purse, and went back to the living room, where my father was still quizzing Steven.

"What do your parents do for a living? You have to be almost rich to live in Park Slope," Daddy was saying.

"We live in a brownstone that my grandparents own. My parents aren't rich," he said, laughing nervously.

"So, what do your parents do for a living?" Daddy asked him again.

"My dad works for Con Edison, and my mom is a professor at Medgar Evers College."

They may not have been rich, but they sure made a lot more money than a bus driver. When Steven and I stepped outside, he removed his car keys from his pocket. "Is this your Station wagon?" I asked, surprised.

"No, my dad lets me use his car," he said grinning. Steven opened the door for me, and I got in. While he walked around to the other side, I quickly scanned the car. It had been freshly vacuumed, and one of those citric air fresheners was hanging from the rearview mirror.

This was my first date; it would have been an understatement to say I was nervous. I was beyond nervous! As we pulled away from the curb, I wished

I had taken that swig of gin. *Just breathe. Just breathe. It's going to be all right.*

"Have you heard this song yet?" Steven asked, putting in a tape. Earth, Wind, and Fire's "Shining Star" began playing.

"Yeah, I like that song! But it's not new. It came out last year."

"When they come to New York, would you like to go and see them?"

"Sure!" I happily replied.

Was he asking me to be his girlfriend? I wasn't sure, but it sounded like he was. If Steven were asking me to be his girlfriend, he would eventually want to kiss me and maybe even have sex with me. I wasn't sure if I could deal with that right now. *I really wished I had taken that swig of gin!* The movie "Sparkle" was playing. After paying for our tickets, we stopped at the concession stand to get a bucket of popcorn and sodas. I asked, "Can I have some Raisinettes?"

"Sure, whatever you want."

After the movie was over, we made our way back to Steven's parked car. We went to White Castle's and ordered some burgers and fries to go. When I got home, daddy was watching wrestling on TV. I was glad he was back. He invited Steven to come in, but he told Daddy he had to get home. Steven thanked me for going to the movies with him, kissed me on the cheek, and left. A perfect gentleman!

I went straight to my room, put on my pajamas, and made some popcorn so I could watch TV with my daddy. As soon as he left the room, I took a big swig of his drink.

"Tell me about your date," Daddy said when he returned.
"We went to see this movie called "Sparkle."
"What happened to my drink?" he asked when he picked it up and noticed that half of it was gone.

"I just sat down, so don't ask me. We ate White Castle's burgers and fries in the car on the way home. The end!"

"I hope you had a good time. He seems like a good kid." I agreed!

12

I HAD GOTTEN USED TO HAVING a drink before going to bed, one when I woke up, and throughout the day. It took the edge off. That's what I needed at the time, something that would take the edge off. At school, no one was the wiser. I didn't participate in class, but I made A's and B's. I was good at pretending to listen when actually, I was only trying to breathe.

If Steven wanted to hang around me, I knew it was going to be hard. Eventually, he was going to see I was not functioning at my fullest capacity. I always felt like I was on the verge of crying and just wanted to avoid human interactions at all costs. But this guy took my indifference to mean I was playing hard to get.

He slipped a card on my desk and brought me a poem
he had written. Since it seemed as if he wasn't going to leave me alone, I accepted another date with him. I intended to tell him when he dropped me off I was not interested in developing a relationship, that I just wanted to be left alone. There had to be other girls at school who would love to spend time with Steven. He was tall, handsome, athletic, and smart.

He requested I dress casually because we were just going to hang out at his house. "Are your parents going to be there?" I asked.
If they weren't, I wasn't going!
"Of course, they're going to be there, silly," he said, playfully bopping me on the head.

Their brownstone was beautiful! It was neat, clean, and smelled like cinnamon. His parents were sitting in the den, watching television. Both of his parents were tall. His mom was wearing a long African print dress, and she had a ring on her big toe. There were several wooden beaded bracelets on both of her wrists. She wore wooden earrings that hung down almost to her shoulder. She had the same smooth complexion as Steven and the same smile. His dad's head was shaven, but his beard made up for him not having any hair on his head. His beard was thick, full, and nearly to his chest. They stood up to meet me, shook my hand, and smiled warmly. "It's nice to meet you," they both said. "We've heard so much about you," his mother said.

I know now that I was supposed to be flattered, but at the time, I was trying to remind myself of something more important. *Just breathe!*

I followed Steven to another den, where his two younger brothers were playing a game of checkers. They were ten years old and eleven, but looked as if they could have been twins. All of them had the same beautiful, smooth skin. They both looked up, surprised. "This is my brother, Bobbie, and the other brat is Paul," Steven said, laughing. *Breathe!* "Scat, guys, we're gonna watch TV," he said. They reluctantly took the game with them and left the room. I sat down and put my purse in my lap and tried not to rock back and forth. *Breathe!* "Would you like something to drink? I was going to get us some snacks. You can come with me if you like. "

"Anything is fine. I'll wait," I added. When he left the room, I tried to regain my composure. I didn't think I was going to meet so many people. *Breathe!*

I knew his parents were going to be at home, but I didn't know he had brothers. I needed a drink! I checked my purse to see if I had any gin in anything. I had none. *Breathe!*

"Since I didn't know what you liked to snack on, I got Bugles, Ruffles, dip, popcorn, and a couple of candy bars. I also got some ginger ale," Steven said, interrupting my thoughts. My heart was pounding.

Please, Lord! Help me to calm down. Please! I begged.

"I like all of those things you mentioned," I said, fighting back the tears. "May I use your restroom?" I asked, standing up.

"Sure, it's right across the hall. Are you okay?" I went to the restroom and shut the door, locked, and unlocked it, and locked it again to make sure it was locked. *Breathe!*

I put the lid down on the toilet and sat down, trying to calm myself. Turning on the sink would drown out any sounds I made involuntarily, so I turned it on and counted to ten until I was better. I calmly walked out and went back to the den. Steven stood up when I came into the room.

"Are you okay?" he asked again.

"Yes, I just had a pain in my stomach. But I feel better now, thanks."

"Did you just funk up my bathroom?" he teasingly asked.

I had to smile at him. He was silly, and it helped me to relax. That was all I wanted to do, just relax.

I had to be home at 11:30, and his mother rode with us. All three of us sat in the front seat together.

"Do you live at home with your parents?" Mrs. Marshall asked.

"My mom died when I was nine, so I live with my dad."

I didn't like talking about that and hoped she wouldn't ask me anything else about it.

"I'm sorry to hear that. I know what you must be going through because I lost my mother when I was a young child also. My father's sister raised me. I admire your dad for taking care of you. He's done a fantastic job," she commented and patted me on the leg. *Breathe!*

"Thank you," I said.

"Do you have any siblings?" she asked.

"I have a brother and sister, but they live in North Carolina with our grandparents."

Her favorite song came on the radio, and she made Steven turn it up. "I love this song!" I liked the song, too, and was surprised when she started singing it.

"I really got to use my imagination! Come on, sing it with me, Steven! Come on sweetie, sing it," she said to me.

I joined in quietly singing. She picked up my hand and began to move it around in the air. She got louder, and I also started to sing louder. We were laughing! I was laughing! *I was actually laughing!*

I hadn't laughed like that in years. We sang a couple of more songs that came on the radio, and I had a good time. *I had a good time!* When Steven parked in front of my building, his mom got out, and I slid across the seat to get out.

With both hands on my shoulders, she said, "I had such a great time and hope you will come and visit us again soon." Then, she hugged me! I hadn't been embraced in years! I hugged her back and tried not to start crying.

"Thank you so much. I appreciate that. Good night," I said.

Steven walked me to my door and said, "I'll call you tomorrow." He was about to kiss me when my dad turned on the porch light, startling him. I was so glad for that because I didn't know if I was ready to be kissing a boy yet.

"I'll talk to you tomorrow," I said, going inside quickly. Daddy had gone back to sit down; he was grinning.

"Who was that you were out there hugging?" he

asked.

"That was Steven's mom."

"Is she single?" he asked, smiling.

"No, she is not! Don't you have a woman?" I joked.

"If you want to call her that," he murmured.

I had a long day, so I went to my room to get ready for bed and to think about what a great time I had. Someone hugged me! I couldn't stop smiling. I threw my clothes on the chair and got dressed for bed. I lay down, still smiling, and went to sleep peacefully, no gin!

Steven and I talked the entire time I was making dinner on Sunday. I took the chicken out of the oven and poured the gravy over it. My rice was perfect and so were the string beans. Daddy liked potatoes in his string beans, and when they were done, I turned off the stove and fixed us each a plate of food. After I had eaten dinner, we talked some more. And before I went to bed that night, he called to say good night.

Again, I went to bed and slept great, no gin! I could hardly wait to get to school Monday so I could see Steven. I sat ahead of him in class, but I could feel him looking at me. I liked this guy! We sat in my usual spot, eating lunch.

"Can I come over on Wednesday after school? I could ride home with you," he said.

"I think so," I said, smiling.

"It's good to see you smiling."

"I smile!"

"Now, you do! You didn't always smile," he remarked. *I was breathing!*

I was Steven's girlfriend, and people knew about it! I felt special and loved. When he put his arm around me, I didn't panic, like I thought I would. We held hands. The first time he kissed me, I closed my eyes tightly and prepared for the panic attack I thought would follow. But he was gentle with me, just a small peck on the lips. I stood there with my eyes closed even after he had pulled away.

"Hello? Are you daydreaming again?" Steven interrupted my thoughts.

"I made you some brownies," I said. I removed the container from my backpack and handed it to him.

"Are there nuts in it?" he asked.

"No, I didn't have any."

"Good, I'm allergic to nuts. So, let me see if you can cook." He laughed. He bit the brownie and chewed with his mouth open. I waited for him to say something, holding back my smile.

"These are great! Where did you learn to bake like that?" he asked, putting the rest of the brownie in his mouth. I felt so special! Someone besides my dad loved me! I was so happy I even told him the brownies were from a box of brownie mix!

As Steven and I became closer, I took the gin bottle

out of my backpack. My dad kept an eye on me when Steven was over to my house, and his parents did the same when I was at their home. Steven was very respectful of me. I didn't worry about him trying anything with me that I didn't want to happen. We were only seventeen; we just liked each other's company.

His family invited Daddy and me over for dinner one Sunday. Daddy was nervous and wondered why we had to meet them. "Steven and I might get married one day. You never know," I said, laughing. I helped him pick out a tie; then I went to get dressed.

On the ride to Park Slope, Daddy and I talked about my plans for the future.

"I think Steven and I will get married one day, and maybe have two children. Yeah! A boy and a girl!" I said.

"Married? I thought you wanted to go to college. C'mon baby. You're too young to be thinking about marriage now," he replied.

"Daddy, I'm only kidding! You are so serious!" I laughed.

"That is not funny! You're trying to cause me to have a stroke!" he chuckled.

Daddy and Steven's father got along very well. They went down to the basement while I sat in the kitchen, watching his mom finish dinner. I asked if she wanted me to help her, but she was almost done. The table was set when we arrived. All she had to do was finish a couple of dishes and put the food on the table.

There was a big bowl of salad sitting in the middle of the table. A long platter with baked salmon sat next to it. There were baked potatoes on another plater and all around it were bowls with sour cream, shredded cheese, chives, and fresh bacon bits. She had made garlic bread and it was soaked in butter and herbs. Everything looked delicious.

Steven sat across from me, and I sat next to my

daddy. It felt so comfortable being around his family. After dinner, we all sat in the living room, talking and enjoying the evening. Our parents told embarrassing stories about us when we were little. It all was such a beautiful evening! They stood on the steps waving goodbye to us.

"Did you have fun, Daddy?" I asked as we were driving home.

"Yeah, I did. I like them; they are cool people. I see why you like that young man. He's a good boy," Daddy said.
I smiled to myself. I was so happy!

13

STEVEN AND I WERE SITTING at our favorite spot, eating lunch one day when I noticed he was just picking at his food. "You're not hungry?" I asked.

"I think I'm coming down with the flu or something. I don't feel good," he replied. I touched his forehead, but he wasn't warm.

"Maybe you should start taking something now before it gets any worst."

"I'm going to take something when I get home," he assured me. He was quiet in English class, which was not like him.

That evening when I called to check on him, he was feeling better. But by Friday, he stayed home because he was feeling weak. "Do you want me to come by after school?" I asked.

"No, I don't want you to catch what I have," he said,

sounding weak.

"Well, I'm going to let you get some rest, and I'll call you tomorrow. I love you."

"Love you, too."

When I had a break, I tried reaching him the next day, but no one was home. I tried again later that day, and still, no one answered. When I got back, I tried again. His mom answered the phone just as I was about to hang up.

"Steven is in the hospital. They are going to keep him and run some tests. They have been doing that all day long. They checked for meningitis, the flu, everything you can think of. Let me give you his phone number. Don't stay on the phone with him long; he needs to get some rest," his mom said.

When I called him, I was nervous and had to fight back the tears. "How are you feeling?" I asked.

"I feel okay now because they just gave me some

pain meds. So, if I fall asleep on you, don't take it personally," he said and laughed.

"Okay, I won't. I missed you today. We had a pop quiz in English. I think I aced it. I can come to see you tomorrow."

"That's good. I got to go. Come to see me tomorrow," Steven said, his voice trailing off.

"Okay," I said and waited for him to hang up.

Daddy and I watched TV until I got sleepy, and I went to bed. I prayed that God would heal Steven from whatever was wrong with him. I didn't sleep peacefully that night and got up early the next day, so I could shower, do my chores, and head to the hospital to see Steven.

When I left, Daddy was getting ready to go to the barbershop. As I walked into Steven's room, I noticed his entire family was there. I hugged them all and hugged Steven. They stayed a while, and then they all left, except his mom. She and I played a board game while Steven slept.

"What have the doctors said is wrong with Steven?" I asked.

"They are running some bloodwork and haven't told us what the results are," she said. Her voice was shaking, and I looked at her. She was worried; I could see it. *Breathe!*

The door opened, and three doctors came into the room, looking stern and worried. Mrs. Marshall stood up and reached for my hand. I held it out to her and waited to see what they were going to say. I prayed silently that it was nothing serious.

"Mrs. Marshall, as you know, we ran a lot of tests on Steven. We wanted to be sure about our concerns. Steven has leukemia," one of the doctors said. She gasped. I glanced at Steven to see how he was taking the news. He put his hand to his eyes and rubbed them. I also reached for his hand. *Breathe!*

One of the doctors came and stood beside Mrs. Marshall and rubbed her back. "There's been a lot of progress made with leukemia, and we are going to do everything we can to help your son. I think the first thing we want to do is see if we can find a bone marrow match with his siblings. We'll also enter him on the national registry," he said.

Mrs. Stevens backed up to the chair and slowly sat down. I had to let Steven's hand go, and he reached for me again. I dropped her hand and went to him. I kissed him on the forehead, the cheek, and his hand. "It's going to be okay," I whispered against his tear-streaked face.

The doctors left the room, closing the door behind them. "Do you want me to call Mr. Marshall?" I asked.

"Yes, call him," Mrs. Marshall replied. I dialed his

number and asked Mr. Marshall to please come to the hospital because the doctors had just left, and Mrs. Marshall needed him.

"I'll be there in thirty minutes," he said quickly and hung up without saying goodbye. I called my daddy and asked him to please come to the hospital.

I wanted to run down the hallway screaming, but I had to be strong for Steven and his mother right now. *I **had** to breathe!*

By the time Mr. Marshall and Steven's brothers got to the hospital, Mrs. Marshall had calmed down and was sitting on the side of Steven's bed, rubbing his hand. I excused myself and went to stand outside to wait for my father. I needed him to hug me and tell me to be strong and to pray and to not cry.

I had gone through this with my mother when she got sick. I sucked it up, and I was strong for everyone. I had to go back to that place and get some strength. I had left it all there, and I needed it now. I closed my eyes and prayed.

Daddy and I went home after being there with the Marshall family for a little while longer. They needed time to process all of what was going on, and it would be easier for them to do that if we were not there.

Daddy and I walked to our car, holding hands. I stared straight ahead, trying to just *breathe!* This was the very hospital my mother was in during her fight for her life. I was only seven when she first developed breast cancer. Jimmie and Trina were just toddlers. They had no idea what was going on.

"You have to be a big girl now. You have to be strong for your little sister and brother," Daddy said.

"What do I have to do?" I ask.

"Just be strong," he replied.

As we rode home in silence, I leaned my head

against the window and stared outside. I tried to be strong. Each time I went to the hospital to see Mommy, she didn't look sick to me. She looked beautiful. I thought someone had lied to me, was trying to play a trick on me. But then they operated and removed her breasts. When I saw her after the operation, she looked tired, sick, and I was frightened. She started her chemo treatments after surgery.

The night before she was supposed to come home from the hospital, Daddy told me to help him get the bedroom cleaned.

"Make sure it's spotless. There can't be one speck of dust on anything or your mom can get sick. Dust everything! The window sills, the ceiling fan, the headboard, and the footboard on the bed. Change the sheets and blankets. Spotless! Everything has to be spotless," he said.

I didn't want to be the one responsible for my mother getting sick again, so I worked hard to make sure everything was just as Daddy had said; spotless!

Mrs. Anderson watched us while he went to get her. She also made us a big dinner and a pot of soup for Mommy. When Daddy came up to get us and bring us downstairs to our apartment, I was so excited to see Mommy. I hadn't seen her in several days, and Jimmie and Trina hadn't seen her since she had gone to the hospital. As we entered her bedroom, she sat up with arms spread wide, hugging, and kissing us, so happy to see us.

Jimmie and Trina wanted to sleep in my parent's bedroom because they were afraid that they would wake up, and she wouldn't be home. So, Daddy made a pallet on the floor beside the bed for them. Eventually, they realized she was home for now and went back to their room.

I was bringing Mommy her breakfast one morning, and she was in the mirror without her scarf; she had patches of hair missing and was combing what was left out—seeing her bald head startled me. But I quickly tried to pull it together because I didn't want to hurt her feelings.

She handed me the scissors and told me to cut the hair on the back of her head off. "For real?" I asked hesitantly.

"Yes, just cut it off. It's going to fall out anyway," she assured me. So, I cut it off and threw it all in the trash can. She got Daddy's razor and shaved what was left entirely off. I ran my hand over her smooth head. She smiled, and I smiled back. She was still my beautiful mother. She put on makeup and also let me put on some. That had never happened, so I enjoyed it.

"I think I'll wear my pearl earrings," she said, as she

put them on. I looked in her jewelry box for some that I could wear. She put a pair of gold hoops in my ears, and we made faces in the mirror. She tried to get back into the swing of things, taking over the chores of the house, getting me up, and ready for school. I thought about her throughout the day and couldn't wait to get home to make sure she was still happy and well.

But soon, she was sick again. She had regular chemo treatments. The first couple of days after treatment left her weak and throwing up. She started losing weight and could barely get out of bed. Mommy's cancer had come back! Grandma came to New York to stay with us and take care of us while Mommy was in the hospital. I knew then something was very wrong. The only time Grandma had ever come to stay with us was for quick holiday visits. This time, she came with a big suitcase and shared my room with me.

The day I was told my mother wasn't ever coming back home, I broke away from Daddy's grasp and ran out the door. I was going to run to the hospital and see for myself. He caught up with me, tightly held me, and kept telling me I had to be strong for my siblings. *I had to! Breathe!*

14

WHEN I CALLED THE HOSPITAL before going to bed, Steven sounded like his old self. We talked for over an hour. Just before hanging up, he said, "I love you."

"I love you, too."

I meant it, too. I loved him. I wanted him to get better and live so we could go to college together and get married one day. We could start a business, have children, and grow old together like his parents and my grandparents.

I stared up at the ceiling most of the night, praying, and then getting mad at myself for praying. I had prayed when Mommy was sick and a lot of good that did. Grandma had told me not to feel that way. She said God didn't make us sick. It wouldn't hurt to pray, so I continued to pray for Steven to get better. After school each day, I went to the hospital and sat with him. He hadn't started his chemo treatments yet, so he only looked a little tired. I sat on the bed, read him our assignments, and helped him work on them so he wouldn't get too far behind and not graduate. Sometimes one of his parents would be there. But most of the time, when I stopped by, he was alone because they had to pick up his brothers from school or something.

"This suck!" he said one day.
I leaned back to look at him. "What do you mean?"
"I didn't even get to take you to our senior prom. And you know what happens after the prom!" he said, laughing.

"We can have our own prom, when you get better," I said, lying back in his arms. I didn't like to hear him being discouraged. When he fell asleep, I went home. *Breathe!*

On the subway ride home, I thought about the day we had my mother's funeral. My siblings and I sat in the first row with her white, shiny coffin in front of us. I could see her in there, but I didn't want to believe it was her. I rocked back and forth that entire day and for weeks after that.

That was when Daddy took us to stay with his father's crazy old sister, Aunt Lizzie. She lived in a brownstone on Lafayette Avenue in Brooklyn. She walked around the house always talking to herself and accusing me of moving something and taking her money. She kept us for two weeks, and I called Daddy and told him I was going to run away if he didn't come and get us.

A couple of months later, he took us to another relative's house, and then finally, he took us to North Carolina. I got to see Jimmie and Trina in the summer for a couple of months; then they went back down south. They had gotten so big, and Trina had developed a southern drawl. I smiled, thinking about her. She looked just like our mother. I wondered if that is why Daddy didn't want us around; we reminded him of our mother. No! That wasn't it!

When I got home, I cleaned up a bit and finished my homework. And like most nights, I talked on the phone with Steven until he went to sleep. I knew they were going to start the chemo soon, and he would be too sick to talk to me. By then, the school would be out, and I could spend all day long with him.

I graduated in June, and Steven was still in the hospital. His parents and my dad came to my graduation. Afterward, we got takeout food and went to the hospital to congratulate Steven because he also had enough credits to graduate. His diploma was hung above his bed, and he had flowers and cards everywhere. Our parents had gotten us a cake, and I stuck a candle in the middle for us to blow out together. He was too weak to blow it out alone. I could tell he was trying to be cheerful and be a part of the festivities, but he looked tired.

When Steven started his leukemia treatment to help it go into remission, he was in the hospital for over a month. By the time he got out of the hospital and returned home, I had learned to play one song on the violin. I was excited for him to hear me; I rushed over to his house, proudly carrying my new violin in its case.

Steven had lost all of his hair! *Breathe!*
I kissed him on his bald head and gave him the flowers I had gotten from the corner vendor. His mom put them in a vase and placed them on his dresser.

"What do you have in that case? Tell me you didn't bring that over here to make me sicker!" he teased.

"I have. You know, I play very well," I said, removing my violin. I sat down on his bed and adjusted my violin under my chin. "Ready?"

He sat there, smiling. "Go on!" he said.

I began playing; my eyes trained on him. He was surprised by my skills. I finished my song and waited for my applause. "Look at you!" he said. I hugged him and put the violin to the side so we could talk.

"I got an acceptance letter today," he said.

"Really? Which college?"

"Morehouse. Maybe you will get accepted at Spellman, and we can go down together."

I lay my head on his chest. I hoped so. *Breathe!*

"I love you, girl," he said, stroking my hair.

"I love you, boy," I replied.

My chest started hurting; I quickly sat up. *Breathe!*

"I'll be right back," I managed to say. I hurried to the bathroom, locked the door, turned on the light, the sink, and tried to catch my breath. *No! No! No!*

Breathe! Just breathe! One, two, three, four, five, six! One, two, three, four, five!

I wiped the sweat from my face and went back to Steven's bedroom. "Did you funk up my bathroom again?" he asked.

"Shut up!" I said, laughing.

Each day I went to his house to help his mom take care of him. Sometimes he had a good day and would be up. I looked forward to those days. I helped him get dressed; we sat in their backyard and smelled the flowers planted out there. Soon his good days outweighed his bad, and he seemed to be back to normal. Rarely was he in bed. He was ready to go to Atlanta and attend college. I had gotten accepted at Spellman. So, Steven and I would be able to see each other every day without our parents being there.

My dad couldn't stand to ride down with the

Marshall's and me, so we said our goodbyes the day before. We went to see a play on Broadway and had dinner at the Horn of Plenty. I couldn't believe he had planned all of this and kept it a secret from me.

I was so excited I couldn't even sleep the night before. I stayed up and watched TV all night long. When the Marshalls came to get me, I was lying on the couch, dozing in and out of sleep. Daddy had taken all of my bags to the van before waking me up.

"I'll call you when I get there," I assured him. He was crying, tears rolling down his cheeks. "I am so proud of you. Your mom would be proud of you, Sweetie. I can't believe this day is happening. I love you," he said, still crying.

As we pulled away from the curb, I looked back at Daddy. He was crying hard, slumped over. It broke my heart. *Breathe!*

Steven reached for my hand and patted it gently. I looked at him, sitting there with a head full of big beautiful hair, looking healthy, and I thanked God for it. I kissed him on the cheek, and his dad reminded us that we were not alone!

His parents thought it best to get Steven settled into his dorm before taking me to Spellman, and that was just fine with me. We carried his things to his dorm room, where his roommate was already there with his parents. I was happy for Steven!

Everything was finally going as we had planned. I knew his cancer was only in remission, and it could come back one day. But for this day right here, I had to think positively. Seeing Steven smiling and happy nearly made me forget he had been at death's door just a year ago.

15

DADDY CALLED TO TELL ME that Jimmy and Trina were moving back to New York. Grandma had a stroke and was headed to a nursing home; Grandpa was also going there.   Daddy was going to get a larger apartment not far from our old apartment. They had been living in North Carolina for eight years, and it was going to be a bit of a culture shock for them having to get back into the grind of New York.

I worried more about Trina than I did Jimmie. I knew from overhearing conversations with Grandma and Daddy that she was boy crazy, and Grandma was having a hard time keeping her sane! I wondered if the constant friction at home contributed to Grandma's stroke. Whatever the cause, I knew

Daddy would be able to get her back on the right track. There was a big difference between down south and the Big Apple.

The day after they arrived in New York, I called Daddy to see how things were going. He put Trina on the phone. "What's up, little sister?" I asked cheerfully.

"Not much, how are you?" she asked in her thick southern drawl. I had to laugh at her! "Whatcha laughing at?"

"Your voice! You are so country!" I teased.

"Whatever. Here is your father," she said and gave the phone to daddy.

"What's wrong with her? I was only kidding about her southern accent, and she got mad."

"She'll be okay. Let me call you tomorrow. We're getting ready to go out and eat. You take care and tell Steven I said hello," Daddy said. Something was not right!

Steven and I were doing well in school. We weren't able to see each other every day as we hoped, but we got to talk on the phone several times each day. He was enjoying school and decided he wanted to pledge a fraternity. I thought the strenuous activity would cause his cancer to come out of remission, but I said nothing because I wanted him to be happy. Everything he wanted to do with his life, I felt he should be able to do, and I wasn't about to stop him. I loved him and wanted him to be happy.

After Steven pledged Alpha, I rarely saw him. Our primary contact for the second year of school was when we traveled home together on the holidays and our daily phone calls. By the third year, we had more time for each other, as our study load wasn't so heavy. Things got better during our final year; we were able to see each other a lot more frequently.

Like any couple spending as much time together as

we did, it was inevitable that we would eventually make love to each other. It was worth the wait. I loved him so much; I knew beyond a shadow of a doubt he loved me, too. We planned to spend the rest of our lives together. We often said it. But I believe, deep down, we knew his cancer could come back anytime, and that made us even closer and valued our time more.

In 1986 Daddy called me to tell me that Trina had dropped out of community college, she disappointed daddy by moving in with a guy who was ten years older than she was. Daddy had spent so much time away that she felt like he didn't have the right to tell her what to do.

"She's lost her mind! I'm only telling her for her own good. I met this cat, and he isn't any good!" Daddy told me.

"The more you tell her to stay away from him, the

more she is going to want to be with him, Daddy. You know how teenagers are," I said, trying to reason with him.

"I didn't have that problem with you!" he reminded me.

"Daddy, I was different. Don't compare me to anyone else," I said. If only he knew that I spent 99% of my teen years drunk.

The same year Jimmy graduated, he returned to North Carolina because he didn't like the big city. He often said he was just a country boy. Jimmy returned to North Carolina and enrolled in Winston Salem State University.

Daddy was living in his big, three-bedroom apartment all alone. He decided to keep the apartment in case his children returned to the nest. That return came a year after Trina left. She called Daddy to ask him to come to get her because Teddy, her boyfriend, had beaten her up. Daddy loaded up his pistol and went to the Bronx to rescue her. He was shocked when she came out of the building, bruised, battered, and pregnant! It was a good thing Teddy wasn't home, or my father would have certainly hurt him.

Daddy called me when he had gotten home from the hospital with Trina. I heard the worry in his voice. I promised him that I would come home for a couple of days at the end of the month. Until then, I decided to call home more often and talk to Trina.

The day I decided to visit, Steven drove me to the airport. I promised to call him as soon as my flight landed. We kissed like I was going off and never returning.

When I stepped out of the cab, Trina was waiting for me on the stoop. She was beautiful but seemed to be lost. I gave her a big hug. As we went upstairs to our apartment, I held her hand.

Daddy was at work. She and I had a chance to sit and talk and catch up. She was seven months pregnant but looked as if she was about to pop that baby out right then. Trina told me that she had met Teddy when she was working a temp job at New York Life. He was a computer programmer for the company and had an apartment in the Bronx.

"He said all of the things that I had waited to hear. He didn't mean any of them, but he sure knew how to say them," she said, laughing.
"What does he think about the baby?" I asked.
"He doesn't care, sis," she said sadly.
I let her know that Daddy and I would be there for her and the baby; she could count on us. *Breathe!*

I had just gotten a financial aid refund check. I took her shopping for some cute maternity tops and some things for the baby. On Sunday morning, I was heading back to the ATL. At the airport, the three of us, Trina, Daddy, and I hugged.

As I sat in my seat by the window, looking out over the clouds, I thought about my mother. I wondered how different her children's lives would have been had she lived. I missed her dearly! *Breathe!*

Steven was waiting for me at the airport, grinning from ear to ear when he saw me. On the ride back to campus, I told him about the things going on with my sister.

"Well, at least she's back at your dad's and we know he isn't going to let anything happen to her," he replied.

As he was coming up the stairs, he gasped stopped, and bent over. "What's wrong?" I asked.
"I've been having these pains in my legs and hip," he said.

"Have you been to the infirmary?"

"No, it's nothing serious."

"I think you need to make an appointment to go to the doctor to be sure," I suggested.

He tossed and turned all night long. First thing Monday, we were in the emergency room. After telling the nurse he was a cancer patient, they immediately took him back. I sat beside the bed, holding his hand and trying to make conversation about things other than the possibility his cancer may be out of remission.

We were in our senior year of school with just two months left before graduation. We were so close! A doctor finally came in and talked with us. Steven was admitted to the hospital. I stepped out to call his parents. They told me they would be on the next flight to the ATL. I returned to the room as the doctor was leaving.

Steven was getting settled into his room. I was a nervous wreck, but I tried to remain calm for him. Four hours after he was admitted, his parents showed up, and I was relieved. I firmly hugged his mom and wiped the tears from her face. We held hands, and his father led us in prayer. I felt somewhat better after that.

The doctor was telling us what treatment plan they wanted to start. But his parents wanted to have him back at New York Presbyterian Hospital. The next morning, Steven was released, and we flew to New York. I was still confident he was going to be okay and go into remission again. This time the doctors decided to do a stem cell transplant, and though he was frail the first couple of weeks, Steven began gaining his strength.

A month later, he was released from the hospital. I had returned to school at his urging; only I couldn't concentrate that well. I asked my academic advisor if it were possible for me to take my final exam now so I could return to New York. "You don't have to take your finals. You have a 4.3 GPA; you can graduate now. Steven has a 4.1 GPA; he can graduate now, too," she said. I secretly hoped he would be well enough to walk across that stage!

I packed up and returned to New York. Trina went into labor the same day I got home. Daddy had gone to the supermarket to shop for the week. Trina and I were watching TV when she cried out in pain. "What's wrong?" I asked alarmed.

"The baby just somersaulted," she said, with a hand on her stomach. Trina got up and went to the kitchen to get something to drink, and I heard her cry out again. I rushed to the kitchen and found her standing in a small puddle of water. "Did your water just break?" I asked, my heart pounding. I called 9-1-1, and we were on our way to the hospital.

I called Daddy to let him know we were going to Mount Sinai. Trina was still moaning and groaning in pain when Daddy showed up. She had squeezed my hand during each contraction; it had cramped up and was now numb. I switched chairs with him to let him deal with the pain for a while.

Finally, she decided to have an epidural. Six hours later, she gave birth to a beautiful little girl that she decided to name after our mother, Cecilia. After they settled into their room, I went to a payphone in the hospital and called Mrs. Marshall.

I told her that I was on my way over; I had to wait for Trina to have the baby. *Breathe!*

Steven was sleeping soundly when I finally got to the hospital. I gently kissed him on the lips. His parents had gone down to the cafeteria and returned with their dinner. To have the stem cell implant, Steven was going to have to go through several rounds of chemo and radiation. This was going to be more aggressive because his body was going to have to go through conditioning to prepare it for the stem cell transplant. I listened as his parents explained it to me and hoped everything would turn out well. I looked at Steven sleeping peacefully and wondered why this had to happen to him. *Breathe! Please! One, two, three! One, two, three! One!*

As I listened to his mother talking, I began feeling overwhelmed. I was going to be able to graduate without having to take my final exams; the flying back and forth from Atlanta to New York; Trina having the baby the same day that Steven was going through these major rounds of chemo and radiation! I could see Mrs. Marshall's mouth moving, her hands waving in the air as she talked. Trina's water breaking, the baby being born. My heart began racing. I was having difficulty breathing. I got up and excused myself and left the room. I ran down the hall, trying to find a bathroom. I ducked into it and closed the door. I locked it and turned on the sink as fast as the water would flow, and I held on to the basin. *Breathe! Just Breathe! One, two, three, four, five! Oh, God! Help me! One, two, three! One, one, one! Just breathe! Breathe! One, one, one!*

I splashed cold water on my face and dried it off with a paper towel. I had to get home! I went back to the room and told Mrs. Marshall I needed a nap and was going home for a couple of hours or so. "He'll be okay tonight. You can come back tomorrow. Just get some rest," she said and hugged me goodbye.

I had done some research. I knew that with the stem cell transplant, Steven was going to be very sick for several weeks. I had braced myself for it, but I wasn't sure if Mrs. Marshall had done the same. *Breathe!*

On Sunday, Daddy and I were in the kitchen fixing dinner when someone rang the buzzer. Trina was laying around, as usual, with her daughter crying her heart out. We both thought she would get the buzzer since she knew we were busy. But whoever it was continued pressing the buzzer! I dried my hands and went to get the door. As I passed, she was sprawled out on the sofa, her daughter was lying in the car seat in front of her, crying, and she was doing nothing.

"Who is it?" I shouted angrily.

"Teddy!" he replied. Trina sat up quickly and smoothed her hair down as if he could see her.

"That's for me!" she said, bouncing from the sofa and running to the door to take over the conversation.

Her daughter was three months old, and she hadn't heard from his sorry behind since the night he had beaten her five months ago when she was seven months pregnant. "Ask him what does he want," I said.

"He wants to see his child and me," she snapped. "Come up, Teddy," she said sweetly and ran to her bedroom to change clothes.

I returned to the kitchen, leaving CeeCee on the floor, still crying. "You need to see why your daughter is screaming!" I said.

"Who was it?" Daddy asked as I returned to the kitchen.

"Teddy," I replied.

Daddy sighed loudly and put the cabbage in the pot with the smoked ham hocks. When Teddy rang the doorbell, Trina yelled for me to get the door and to bring her the baby. I took CeeCee to her bedroom first. Trina was jumping up and down, trying to get her post-pregnancy body into a pair of jeans that were already tight pre-pregnancy! *Breathe!*

I had never met Teddy. All I knew about him was that he was violent and older than my sister. Once I opened the door and saw this tiny little man who appeared to be at least my Daddy's age, I was shocked. "Yes, may I help you?" I asked.

"I'm Teddy. I came to see Trina." I stepped to the side to let him in, and he nervously stepped into the foyer.

"Have a seat; she'll be out in a few minutes."

He sat down on the sofa, smoothed his pants down, turned his watch face up, and took off his sunglasses. Daddy entered the room; Teddy stood up and introduced himself to Daddy. I could see he was visibly nervous. Daddy had been cutting up the baked chicken and was still holding the knife.

Trina rushed into the room because she was afraid that Daddy was going to say something to hurt Teddy's feelings. She didn't know our father. He had drilled into me that people are who they are. They will treat you the way they've always treated everyone they've ever dealt with. You have control over how someone treats you. If you don't want to be treated with disrespect, leave them alone. Trina obviously wasn't aware of that information. She stood there holding the baby, now quiet in her arms as if she were the doting mother.

Teddy went to her and took the baby from her arms, smiling. "She is beautiful! Oh, my goodness!" he murmured.

"Where have you been, brother?" Daddy asked him. Cecilia was three months old. As far as Daddy was concerned, he was at least three months late getting here to see his child.

"I—I," he was trying to explain. Then Trina interrupted him, saying, "He's here now, Daddy."
I threw the towel I was holding over my shoulder and returned to the kitchen. I couldn't watch this foolishness.

A month later, I came home from the hospital after

visiting Steven to find that Trina and her daughter had moved out and gone to live with Teddy in the Bronx again. She left her bedroom looking a hot mess. I knew Daddy would have a fit when he got home.

I changed clothes, cleaned her room, and remade the bed with fresh linen. I was tired and so drained.
In two weeks, Steven was due to walk across the stage at Morehouse to receive his degree. We flew down to Atlanta for the ceremony. The morning of graduation, Daddy, I, and Steven's family was sitting in the arena waiting until we heard Steven Luther Marshall, III so that we could cheer for him. I could hardly believe it! I stood there, tears in my eyes, unable to even hold the camera to take his photo. He looked handsome and healthy that day.

A week later, my degree arrived in the mail. I didn't need to walk across the stage, just having the diploma was good enough for me. Besides, I didn't want to take away from the miracle of Steven getting his degree. *Breathe!*

So far in my life, everyone I had ever met had taken first place in my life. I had stepped back to allow others to shine, to get what they wanted, to be the center of attention. I had lost my worth and didn't even have the strength to look for it or to even recognize when I found it.

I hung my degree above my graduation picture and stood there, admiring it. *Mommy would be proud of me.* She always knew her children would be okay because she trusted and believed in Daddy. Maybe she had placed too much trust in him. He was only one person, and though he did his best with us, at some point as adults, his children had to take responsibility for our own actions. It was that, or either "it" didn't trickle down to Trina.

I sat down and closed my eyes for a second. At that

moment, it seemed I received a flashback of my entire life. The pain hit me in the chest as if someone had punched me. I leaned forward, trying to catch my breath. I couldn't do this right now! It was almost time for Daddy to be getting home from work, and I had to start fixing dinner. *Breathe! Breathe!*

I made my way to the bathroom and splashed water on my face. *Breathe!* I sat down on the lid of the toilet and leaned forward. I felt faint and anxious all at the same time. *Oh, God! Please, help me!*

I was going to need a drink. I poured some gin into a juice glass and took a sip. Angry now, I threw the glass and remaining liquor into the sink. I could not carry my load and everyone else's! I was tired of trying to do it! It was not my responsibility! Damn! Damn! Damn! I fought back the tears. I had to get my father's dinner prepared because he would be home from work shortly. I wiped my face on a paper towel and sucked it up as best as I could. *Breathe!*

16

WITH MY DEGREE IN HAND, I set out to get a career started. I also decided I wanted to get my doctorate. However, I wasn't sure what kind of work I wanted to do at this point. I had to make a living, so I accepted a job in finance and found my way to the World Trade Center.

Steven got job offers from Virginia to Syracuse. When he told me, I tried to be happy for him, but I feared the anger would show on my face. I decided I had better go home. On the subway ride home, I thought about all of the times I had completed his work for him when he was too sick to do it. I smiled when he bragged about getting A's to his family as if he had done his assignments. I was about to cry; my chest hurt, my eyes burned. I was tired! I was so tired! I started rocking back and forth. I felt people staring at me, wondering what my problem was. I had to get off the train at the next stop. I stumbled up the stairs, and once outside, I found myself near a bar. I went inside and sat down.

When the waitress came over, I ordered Chivas Regal on the rocks. She set down a bowl of pretzels and walked away. Soon as she returned with my order, I drank it in one gulp and ordered another. After three of them, I went out, hailed a taxi, and went home. I showered and went to bed, clutching a bottle of Beefeater's Gin. *Breathe!*

While I started my job at Cantor/Fitzgerald's Security on the 104th floor, Steven was basking in the many offers he had gotten because of my hard work, and I was secretly resenting it. I don't know why I couldn't be happy for him. I wanted to be, but I knew the truth. I'm not sure if I wanted him to give me credit for it. I'm not sure if I wanted him to stop bragging about his A's or to acknowledge how much I had helped him. I, too, had graduated with honors, but mine were overlooked because of what was going on with Steven. Later, I felt awful for being jealous of a man fighting to stay alive.

One bright sunny morning, just as I was about to walk out the door headed to work, the phone rang. Daddy had both hands in the soapy water washing the dishes. I shifted my bags to my left and answered the phone. It was Trina; she wanted to know if she could come back home. She said she wasn't happy at Teddy's place. She wanted to return home *again*.

"Do you have carfare?" I asked.

"I lost my job because I couldn't get a babysitter. No! I don't have anything but this baby," she answered.

"Take a taxi, and Daddy will pay when you get here."

"Thank you, Bennie. I love you."

"I love you, too, Trina."

"Daddy, Trina is coming back home. Here is $50 to give the taxi when she gets here. I will talk to you later, love you," I said and kissed him on the cheek. "Have a good day, sweetie," he said.

By the time I got to the subway station, I knew I had missed my train. I waited for the next one with my head stuck in the book I had started reading. When my cell phone rang, I knew without looking that it was Steven. "Morning, babe," he said.
"Good morning. Whatcha doing today?"
"I have to go to the city today and was hoping I could meet you for lunch."
"Sure, call me later," I said.

I boarded the train for work, closed the book, and put it in my bag. A man was standing on the left side of me, reading a *Watchtower* magazine from the Jehovah's Witnesses. The heading read, "Seek Peace and Pursue It." I tried to read what it said, but could only make out a few of the sentences. I eased closer to him to see it. He suddenly looked at me. "I have another one if you would like it," he said.

I sheepishly smiled and nodded. The man reached into his bookbag and gave me the other magazine. I opened it and began reading the article. He then handed me his business card, and I thanked him.

He got off the train and smiled upon exiting. When I got off the train later, my sister called me. She was waiting for me in front of the building. I was surprised because I told her to take a taxi and go home. I went outside to see her standing with Cecelia in a stroller. She was wearing a short denim dress and a large straw hat, hiding her face. I had never worn a dress that short; it barely covered her butt. I didn't want any of my co-workers to see me with her.

I kissed her on the cheek, nearly knocking her hat off. "Come on, let's go get some breakfast," I said, taking over the stroller. I pushed it up the block to the deli. I glanced at my watch, and it was 8:25 a.m. I didn't have to be to work until nine. I had time to eat a bagel and send her on her way to Queens without being late.

Trina wanted to sit down and eat. I got our tray of food and went to sit down. I could tell she wanted to talk, so I was just going to have to be late that morning.

"Are all the men in New York crazy?" she asked.
"I don't think so. You just have to be more selective. What happened?" I asked. "Teddy is just a trip. I can't even fart without him wanting to be there to smell it!" she laughed.
"He's jealous?" I asked, not exactly sure what she was trying to tell me.
"He's crazy jealous!" she exclaimed, her mouth was

full of the breakfast sandwich. "That's how some men are when they get a beautiful woman," I said, trying to make her feel better. She wiped her mouth and smiled. "You'll find someone. You just have to be patient."

Trina broke off a piece of her bread and put it in Cecelia's mouth. CeeCee was getting some teeth at the bottom and hungrily began chewing on the bread.

"What did he do? He didn't hit you, did he?" I asked, sipping my coffee. I added more cream and sugar. She was about to respond when the roar of an airplane sounded very close by.

People in the deli looked around at each other as if to ask, "Why is that plane so close?" Then it was followed by a window shattering boom.

"What was that?" I asked because it sounded like a bomb. I got up and followed the folks outside to see what it was. The plane had flown into the World

Trade Center!

People from the diner, and the street, began running toward the towers; others, near the towers, were running in our direction. I ran back into the deli, grabbed the baby, and my sister's hand. "Come on, let's get out of here," I said, leaving behind the stroller. I didn't know if the building was going to explode.

We went outside and looked up at the building. We saw this massive hole in the side of the building, and smoke billowing out. From the floors above and below, we saw people falling or jumping from the building.

"It's a terrorist attack!" someone running past us cried out. A few minutes after the first plane hit, a second plane crashed into the second building. By then, we were all convinced it was a deliberate act. It had to be terrorists! We ran away from the building. I was gripping my sister's hand, but she wasn't able to keep up with me. I tried to maintain my grip on her, but we got separated. I moved out of the crowd and waited against a building, trying to see if I could see her in the crowd passing. "Trina! Trina!" I screamed, but I didn't see her.

I started running again. The baby was crying now, too. It was like a dream in slow motion. I saw the Watchtower building and noticed some people were heading over the Brooklyn Bridge. I followed them, still looking back for my sister. "Trina! Trina!" I shouted.

Then I heard her calling me. "I'm here!" she yelled. I moved out of the crowd again, and then I saw her. Her hat was no longer on her head. We firmly held on to each other this time and made our way across the bridge.

I looked back at the towers; they were both on fire now. Thick black smoke was billowing from both of the buildings. Then the buildings collapsed! There was another rumble, and the building near them also collapsed.

I heard people screaming everywhere. Dense dark smoke and ash were coming from where the buildings once stood. There was so much noise; sirens from police cars, fire engines, and car horns blowing and people screaming! *Breathe! One, one, one, one! Breathe!*

I opened my phone and called home. I knew Daddy was probably going out of his mind. The call went to voicemail. "Daddy, Trina, and CeeCee are with me. We're heading across the Brooklyn bridge. We are safe. I will call you back! I said, trying hard to sound calm despite the chaos around me.

I also called the Marshalls' and left them a voicemail. I ended each call with, "I love you." *I can't breathe!*

I wanted to get to Queens to see my daddy, to feel the safety of his arms. However, the trains were not running, and car services were afraid to operate. All the boroughs were at a standstill! I couldn't walk to Queens, but that is what Trina and I started doing. New York was in a panic. Every high-rise company had let its employees go home; the streets were full of people. Sirens were heard everywhere.

I thought about my coworkers. I hoped they were all safe, but I knew many of them were not. We had all gotten to work early so we could get breakfast or get the day started early or whatever the reasons were. I knew the planes had hit the upper part of the building. My coworkers had to be affected, even if they were initially just trapped because the elevators were not working. Now that the buildings had collapsed, I knew they were killed. I prayed and prayed as we walked along. Trina kept pulling me along because I kept having anxiety attacks. *I can't breathe!*

It was the longest walk of my entire life. Finally, I saw my neighborhood. I saw my apartment building! I didn't realize I had left my purse until I got to the door and didn't have my keys. I pushed the buzzer. "Daddy, let us in!" I said.

He came running down the stairs and squeezed Trina, Cecelia, and me.

We watched how this was unfolding on the TV. It was then I found out that a plane had hit the Pentagon before the World Trade Center. Another plane, intended for the White House, had been diverted and crashed into a wooded area. It all seemed like a dream. I excused myself and went to my bedroom. I drank a glass of gin and went to bed. *I was too tired to breathe!*

I was sleeping when Steven called. He had been trying to get me all day, but the phones were all down. "I'm fine," I assured him.

"I want to marry you right now! I don't want to wait until we do this or that. Tomorrow isn't promised to any of us. While we have the right now, I want to do this," he said. *Breathe!*

Three weeks later, we stood in his parents' Park Slope brownstone with our families while a minister performed the ceremony. We spent our honeymoon fixing up our new apartment not far from his parent's brownstone. I didn't have a job and was afraid to go to the city to look for another one. I didn't know how many of my coworkers had been killed; people I'd spent the majority of my waking hours with were now gone. Some of them hadn't even been found yet. I was sick to my soul. I was startled by every sound – a cat's meow, a siren, a car horn, a door slamming, a cup dropping, the toast popping up from the toaster.

I was drowning with all of these people around me, and not one person noticed me flailing in the water.

Help me, please, God! I can't do this anymore! I can't breathe!

17

HOWEVER, EACH DAY I GOT up and smiled and went about my day while I was with people. But as soon as I was alone, I fell apart. *I can't breathe!*

I found Dr. Verlonda Whickers in the phonebook. Her practice was located on the second floor of a building in the Bedford/Stuyvesant section of Brooklyn; it was right above a dry cleaner. I took a taxi to her office because I was too afraid to be under the ground on a train. Crowds – I wasn't ready for that! The first day I went to see her, I was nervous. I just sat in the chair, rocking back and forth, running sentences together, and making absolutely no sense whatsoever. I only had forty-five minutes; I didn't pause to take a breath! She was looking at me, holding a pen and pad, but not writing down anything. When my time was up, I thanked her and stood to leave.

"I would like to see you tomorrow," she said, writing on a card.

"What? So soon?" I asked.

"Yes, tomorrow at 11 a.m.," she said. She handed me the reminder card and stood to let me out. I walked out of her office, puzzled. However, by the time I got into a taxi, I knew why she wanted to see me the next day. It sounded like I had lost it!

I returned the next day. I sat on my hands and rocked back and forth as we talked. "Tell me about your parents," she requested. Her voice was soothing, and I wasn't aware of that yesterday. I told her about my father and how he had been such a pillar in my life. I don't know what I would have done without him.

"What about your mother?" she asked. I was trying not to rock back and forth but was not successful.

Breathe!

"My mother died when I was nine from breast cancer," I answered. This time, she was taking notes. Every once in a while, she jotted down something. I shared with her about my mom's butter cookies, her date cake, her pancakes, how she always smelled like love.

"What does love smell like to you?"

"It smells like peace, rain, fresh air, cinnamon. Love," I replied.

"That was beautiful, Benita," she replied, smiling.

"Thank you." I sat back in the seat and placed both hands on my lap.

"Benita, is this your first time talking about your mother like this?"

"Yes," I said and wiped my eyes.

"If you want, we can end the session here, and pick up at your next appointment," she suggested.

"When can I see you again?"

"Would you like to come back this Friday?"

"Yes, I will see you on Friday. Same time?" I asked.

"Friday at 11:00, it is."

I felt as if I had left something in that office. I felt so good I got myself an ice cream sundae.

Steven was in the kitchen, making an early dinner. "I made plans for us to pack a picnic basket and go to Central Park for the free concert this evening. Go put on something comfortable," he said.

I spun around on my heels, hurried straight to our bedroom, and changed into a pair of jeans and a tank top. I was buckling my sandals as he came in to change his shirt. "Ready?" he asked. *Breathe!*

On the way towards the subway station, I thought about our marriage. Since I was home, trying to recuperate from the 9/11 tragedy, I had been on auto-pilot, or should I say Steven pilot? He told me what to do, and I did it. I no longer had a mind of my own. We now operated on one brain – his! When did I allow this to happen? Why did I let this happen?

"Are you ready to ride the subway?" he asked when we were outside.

I looked up at him, trying to calm down. "I'm not going to let anything happen to you," he said assuredly.

I wanted to yell at him, "How do you think you can stop a terrorist attack? How, Steven, I would like to know the answer to that," Instead, I forced what I hoped was a smile and gripped his hand as we walked to the train station. *Breathe! You've got to pray about this, so pray! Just breathe and pray!*

When the train arrived, I firmly held on to Steven. He had to pry my fingers off of his wrist. "Relax, baby," he said and hugged me. *Just breathe!*

We finally made it. I wanted to run up the stairs and

out into the fresh air. It had been a year since the terrorist attacks, and I was still afraid!

As we walked up the block to the park, him carrying our small basket with whatever he had prepared for us in it, and me carrying our blanket, I knew I was going to have to snap out of this funk and get myself together.

I didn't enjoy the concert, and it showed all over my face. I was tired of pretending to like things I didn't like. I was sick of going to places I didn't want to go to. I was exhausted!

Steven wasn't ready to go, and he didn't seem to care when I told him that I was leaving. I walked to the corner and hailed a taxi. "Can you take me to Queens?" I asked.

"Sure, Ma! Get in," the young driver said.

I took a hot shower, fixed some scrambled eggs, and

got my bottle of gin out of the cabinet. I fixed a too stiff gin and juice and lay down on the sofa to watch TV. I was on my second drink when Steven came home. He mumbled a hello and went to our bedroom. Steven finally came out with his pillow and lay down on the opposite end of the sofa. I could tell he was looking at me, but I refused to look in his direction.

"Bennie, I am sorry about tonight. I should have asked if you wanted to go. I apologize," he said.

He started tickling my foot because I was still ignoring him. I tried not to smile, laugh, or react in any way. He picked up my foot and kissed it, and then my ankle. I knew where this was heading.
"I accept your apology. And you need to allow me to make decisions for myself, Steven. Okay?"
"Okay. I apologize," he said again.

I looked at him then. He was only doing to me what

I had allowed to happen this past year while I lay around guzzling gin and feeling sorry for myself. I was glad I wasn't in the World Trade Center that horrible morning, but then, I felt guilty because I wasn't there, and so many of my coworkers were. *Breathe!*

"Do you want to go to bed?" he asked.

"Only if you are going to hold me," I whispered.

18

"TELL ME ABOUT YOUR HUSBAND," my therapist requested at my next visit.

"We have been together for twenty-eight years. He is my first and only love, and I'm his first and only. He was diagnosed with leukemia when he was sixteen, and all these years we have been dealing with it to keep it in remission."

"Are you happy in your marriage?"

"Sometimes, I am. Well, most of the time. This past year-and-a-half has been difficult because, after 9/11, I had many issues that kept me from functioning at 100 percent."

She jotted something in her notes.

"I love him very much. He's my best friend," I said.

She continued to write in her notebook. Dang! I had

never seen her write that much before. She looked up, surprised by my silence.

"Go on," she said.

"I'm ready to get back to my whole self. Independent and everything," I explained. She stopped writing and looked at me. "Steven has been very patient with me. At first, I didn't know how I was going to make it."

"What about now? How do you get back to how it used to be?"

"I don't know."

"Did you like your life better when you were the strong one, and Steven needed you?"

"He still needs me!"

She was pissing me off. She made another note.

"Every couple of years, or so, he has to get another round of chemo treatment to help keep his leukemia in remission. I'm there for him," I said. *Breathe! Just breathe! Why is this chick trying to get my goat? I love my husband!*

"Why did you mention his chemo treatment? Do you feel that is the only way he needs you to be there for just that?" she asked, rolling the pen between her fingers.

"When Steven was in college, I did most of his work because he was always sick or about to get sick. He excelled because of me! He graduated because I was there for him. So, if he has been there for me these couple of years, so what?" I snapped. She jotted down something quickly. I sighed loudly.

"What motivated you to do his school work? Did he ask you to?"
"He didn't have to ask me. I... It was... I just did it."
"How did Steven respond to you doing his work? Did he thank you for that?"

"What difference does it make? He was my fiancé,

and I was helping him to succeed. We had plans; you know."

"Benita, I want you to go home and think about how much you have done for your husband and try to determine for yourself what your motives were. Also, ask yourself if those actions helped your husband, and then, we can talk about it again next week, okay?"

On the ride home, I thought about just that. I helped Steven because if I hadn't, he would have had to come out of school until he got better. And who knew if he were going to get better. I didn't want anything to interfere with our plans for the future. That was why I did his assignments and helped him as I did.

He would have graduated, anyway, at some point. He was an intelligent man. *Breathe, Bennie!*

I had never had to depend on anyone. I was always

the one doing for others. For thirty years, I had been the one always doing for other people. I didn't know how to let others do for me. I resented it! I resented that my husband was the sole breadwinner in the house, paid all of the bills, and took care of us during this time I was recuperating. I had done the same for him throughout our marriage, and it made me feel important. I was squeezing the pole so hard I thought I would pull it up from the floor of the train!

My chest starting hurting; I felt horrible. I could not have a panic attack on this train. *Count! One, two, three, four! One, two, three, four! One, two, three, four!*
I arrived home, took some Tylenol, and went to bed. I set the alarm to wake me in an hour. That would give me enough time to vacuum and fix dinner before Steven got home from work.

I didn't hear the alarm! I jumped up and frantically tried to get myself together so I could at least throw something in a pot right quick before Steven got home.

I had forgotten to take something out to cook! I sent him a text message to see where he was. "I'm just getting on the subway. What's up?" he texted back. "Nothing. See you when you get here."

I had enough time to run to the Jamaican café around the corner and get something from there. I ordered the Jerk chicken, peas and rice, and steamed cabbage. I got a cake from the bakery and came home. I put the food in the oven and ran the vacuum. I was just putting it away when I heard the keys in the lock.

I went to the kitchen to set the table. "Hey, baby," I said, leaning in to get my kiss.

"Let me get this subway smell off, and I will be back for dinner," he said, releasing me.

I finished setting the table and began plating the food; the shower turned off, and I poured each of us a glass of wine. "That looks good, baby," Steven said. I would have lied and said I cooked it, but the containers were in the trashcan.

"How was work?" I asked. Generally, I only half-listened, but I decided to listen today as he told me about the secretary for his department and her affair with one of their coworkers. I laughed when he shared a joke.

"What did you do today?" he asked.

"I had an appointment to see my therapist, Dr. Verlonda. Then I came home and took myself a nap!"

"How is therapy going?"

"I'm getting there."

"I knew you would."

"I talked to Daddy today, too, and told him I would get over there tomorrow, and we can go and have lunch someplace, or maybe we will go see Trina," I said.

Trina had purchased an attached home in Bed-Stuy when they were offering the Jeremiah loans to residents. The Jeremiah loans helped single parents who had never purchased a home before obtain financing. The loans were low interest and required little or no money down. She was a receptionist at a doctor's office now. She seemed to be doing well; however, Daddy still worried about her, though. If she had been living with him, he would not be worrying so much about her. She was a grown woman!

As I walked up to her building, several people were sitting on the steps. They didn't move until we asked them to. I held onto Daddy's hand as we walked past them.

Trina had cooked a pot of black-eyed peas, rice,

biscuits, and baked chicken. Daddy was very impressed with her cooking skills; said it tasted just like his Mama's cooking. He was acting as he had never had anything as good as what she had made. When I lived at home, I used to cook most of our meals, and not once did I ever remember him going on and on about a pot of freaking black-eyed peas! I was so mad! *Breathe!*

I was upset; I didn't even want to eat anything. It was petty, but then I was so outdone by the jealous feelings I had that I was sorry I even came with Daddy to visit her. Instead of enjoying any of her meal, I went to Cecelia's room to hang out with her while Daddy and Trina ate.

When I got home, I called my therapist. "Benita, I can make an appointment for you to come and see me on Thursday, but I can't talk to you right now," she interrupted me.

"I've cooked him all kinds of wonderful meals, and he was going on and on about a pot of black-eyed peas and rice! I don't care what I do for people, no one seems to appreciate the things that I do! I am so tired!" I was on a full-blown rant.

"How about I miss lunch, and we can meet tomorrow, but right now, I really can't talk to you. I will put you down for noon, okay?"

"Okay, noon it is!" I hung up and caught a glimpse in the mirror of myself. I looked just like a raging lunatic! I smiled at myself. I was losing it! I started laughing so hard that I started choking. *I was losing my mind!*

To prove I could make better black-eyed peas than my sister, I sorted a bag and set them on the back of the stove to soak overnight. I would put them in the crockpot with a ham hock and take them to Daddy's house while I was out. That was my plan. But by the next morning, I realized it was childish!

As I walked into my therapist's office, I didn't even wait for my butt to hit the chair before I started laughing. I told her about my silliness the day before. The entire time I spoke, she looked at me as if I were crazy.

"I am glad you realized it was not that serious. But since you're here, did you get a chance to think about what we discussed at our last meeting?" she asked, picking up her notepad and pen.

Oh yeah, I was supposed to think about why I helped Steven and what my motives were.

I shifted in the seat and tried to get comfortable. "I did think about it, and I helped Steven because we had plans for our lives. We were going to go to school and get our degrees and come back to New York and get these high paying jobs, and then we would start a family. We were going to live happily ever after." I sat on my hands and tried to count to myself so that I didn't rock back and forth.

She jotted down a note. I was waiting for her to say something. She removed her glasses and wiped them with a tissue. "So, do you mean you helped him so your plans would be successful?"

"Yes, and I wanted us to stay on point, you know. I was scared too that he would come out of remission and then have to start all over."

"I want you to think about this before answering, okay. Did the possibility that Steven would not make it have a role in what you were doing?"

I was nervous, and try as I might, I started rocking back and forth. She wrote in her notebook. *Breathe!*

"Yes. I was afraid he would die before our lives together started," I finally managed to say. She smiled and stopped writing. I reached for a tissue and wiped the tears from my eyes.

"Why didn't the two of you have children? Did you not want any?"

Steven and I did want children.

"We tried to get pregnant three years after we were married. Everything was going well then. Steven was in remission and had been for six years. We had a lovely home, some money saved, and we were ready. We kept trying and trying, but nothing happened. We finally went to a fertility specialist who ran tests on both of us. We were never told the chemotherapy would cause Steven to become sterile. We would never be able to conceive a child together."

"How did you take that news?"

"I was disappointed, of course. But what was I going to do? It wasn't going to change things." She wrote a long sentence, and I watched, wishing I could read what she was writing. *Breathe, Bennie!*

"When would you like to come back, Benita? Wednesday and Friday, I have openings at 4:00 p.m."

"Wednesday is fine." She wrote my appointment on a card, stood up, and handed it to me. I took the card and thanked her. "Benita, when you come back next week, I want you to let me know if you think a small dose of an antidepressant will help you to feel better. If so, I can refer you to my partner. His office is just down the hall from me. He's a psychiatrist."

"Are you tired of seeing me?" I was startled by her suggestion.

"No, I'm not tired of seeing you. I just think that medication can take some of the edge off, make you feel more relaxed," she explained.

"I'll think about it."

I wasn't taking any medication! I wasn't that bad. I just needed someone to talk to, to help me have breakthroughs and be able to sort things out. *Medication! She must be the crazy one!*

19

STEVEN AND I WERE SITTING IN his oncologist's office, waiting to hear the results of the tests. The doctor finally entered the room, holding Steven's chart. He sat on the stool and rolled over toward us. "I have some bad news. We found some cancer cells in your blood work. We want to get you back in here, start the chemo," he said.

I squeezed Steven's hand. "Are you sure?" I asked hopelessly.

"Yes, we're sure. We'll give you a couple of days to get prepared. Do you want to shoot for this Friday or Saturday?" he asked Steven.

I looked at my husband's facial expression, hoping to be able to read something. He let go of my hand and stood up, "Friday is good for me."

Friday was good! Girl, you better breathe! This is Steven's decision, not yours. Breathe!

I reached for his hand again as we walked to the elevator. He looked down at me and smiled, patted my hand, then kissed it. "We're gonna make it through this," I said.

"No doubt, no doubt!" he said, smiling. This would be our first time out of remission in several years. I didn't know what to expect, but I knew I needed my husband.

We told our parents what was going on in person. They were positive, supportive, and said they would go with us to the hospital on Friday.

After Steven fell asleep that night, I went into the living room to be alone. I had nervous energy and decided to organize the kitchen cabinets. After I was finished with that, I rearranged the things on the shelving in the living room. I ran across the *Watchtower* magazine the man on the train gave me the same day of the terrorist attacks on the World Trade Center nearly fifteen years ago. I put it on the kitchen counter so I would remember to read it the next day. I noticed a scuff mark on the kitchen floor; I took out the mop and cleaned the floor.

By the time I returned to bed, it was three in the morning. I kissed Steven on his cheek and moved closer to him. I started praying. I wasn't good at it, but I wanted God to know I needed him; *we* needed him.

On Friday, our parents met us at the Memorial Sloan-Kettering Cancer Center. After checking in and filling out the many forms, we went upstairs to Steven's room. He went to the bathroom to change; his mom came to sit with me and asked me how I was holding up.

"I'm good, thanks," I lied. She kissed me on the cheek. I remembered I had an appointment with my therapist at 4 o'clock that afternoon. I could not miss this appointment! I needed it more today than at any other time!

Steven was settled in bed and watching TV. They weren't going to start the chemo until the next morning. I said, "Steven, I have an appointment. I'll be back in a couple of hours." I kissed him goodbye and hurried to the subway. The train was just pulling into the station, so I ran to get it and sat down by the door.

There weren't that many people in the car I was in, and I was glad of that. I could rock back and forth and not worry about what others were thinking of me. *One, two, three, four, five! One, two, three, four! One, two, three, four, five! Get it together! Bennie, you can do this!*

I rushed to my therapist's office and dashed up the stairs. I sat down and started crying like a baby. She reached out, holding the box of tissue to me. I took several, wiped my eyes, and blew my nose.

"What's going on, Benita. Tell me! What has happened?" she asked.

"My husband was admitted to the hospital this morning. He is not in remission anymore, and he has to have chemotherapy again. We have to do this all over again," I cried.

"You could have missed this appointment, I would have understood," she said softly.

"I had to come. I needed to see you." I hadn't planned to, but I decided at that moment that it might be helpful if I got some medication. Secretly, I was only going to take it when I needed it. I didn't want something I had to take every single day. Before I got a chance to tell her that, she suggested it again. "I will be willing to see a psychiatrist, yes," I replied.

She excused herself. Upon returning a few minutes later, she had a tall, good-looking man with her. He appeared to be my age. I stood up and was introduced to him. "Benita Marshall, this is the doctor I was telling you about. This is Dr. Sekou Thomas." He firmly shook my hand and smiled, showing beautiful perfect teeth.

"If you like, Benita, I can schedule an appointment to meet with you tomorrow. I work on Saturdays from 8:00 – 1:00 p.m. I have an 8:00 and an 11:00 a.m. available."

I chose the 8:00 a.m. appointment because I wanted to see him as soon as possible. Seeing him early meant I would have the rest of the day set aside to be with my husband.

I stayed at the hospital until Steven fell asleep at nine. I told him that I was going to go home and sleep, but I would be back the next morning at 9:30 or 10 o'clock. We kissed goodnight; I took a taxi and went home.

There was an eerie silence at home. I turned on the lamp in the living room and took a hot bath. I decided to sleep on the sofa instead of in our bed. I fixed a hot cup of tea and lay down on the couch. In the distance, I heard a cat outside. I had never been in a place alone before. I started wishing I had gone to spend the night in Queens with my Daddy. I called him, not thinking about how late it was.

"I am so sorry, I didn't mean to wake you up," I apologized.

"No, it's okay. How are you doing?" he asked.

"I'm okay. I just wanted to talk. This is the first time I have ever been alone overnight. I was getting scared and wanted to hear my Daddy's voice."

"Ain't nothing wrong with that, baby."

"Have you spoken to Trina lately?" I asked, not that I cared right then. I was more concerned about my husband.

"I talked to her earlier today. She's Trina, what can I

say?" He chuckled.

"It's so quiet without Steven here. I don't know what I would do without him. Daddy, how did you manage when Mommy... when Mommy passed away?"

"I felt just like you do right now. I didn't think I was going to be able to make it without your mother. I had the three of you to take care of, and I just...I prayed a lot. I made a lot of mistakes, too. But I prayed mostly."

I thought about what he said for a few seconds. "I love you, Daddy. I'll talk to you later, okay?"

"Good night, baby."

I turned off the lamp, pulled the covers up around my chin, and fell asleep. There was nothing I could do about Steven being sick again but pray. It wasn't going to do either of us any good for me to mope around and cry. I had to be strong for him. I knew the doctors were going to do everything they could to help him get better, and I had to trust that.

I woke up the next morning at six, I fixed myself a hearty breakfast and read the paper while sipping my coffee. I got dressed and packed up some things I thought Steven might want with him while he was in the hospital. I rode the subway to see Dr. Thomas, arriving just a little past 7:30. The door to his office was locked. I sat down at the top of the stairs. He arrived at 7:45 and was startled to see me there already.

I followed him to his office and sat down while he put on some coffee and turned on his computer. I could tell that Dr. Verlonda had already discussed my case with him. I sat across from him while I briefly told him what was going on with me. He listened, not taking any notes.

"Where do you get your prescriptions filled?"
"CVS on Nostrand Avenue."
"I want you to start by taking just a half pill each morning with a full glass of water and some food. I

will schedule another appointment to come by in two weeks. If you're not feeling any differently, I'll increase it to the whole pill, okay? Do you have any questions?"

"Yes, what are you prescribing me?"

"Zoloft," he replied.

On the train ride to see my husband, I Googled Zoloft and learned the side effects were: diarrhea, dizziness, drowsiness, fatigue, insomnia, tremors, headache, anorexia, decreased libido, and anxiety!

I walked in with feelings of anxiety and depression, and I was prescribed a pill whose side effects caused more anxiety and most of the other symptoms I already had? There had to be something natural to take to help calm folk down.

When I got to the hospital, Steven was playing a game on his cell phone. I kissed him and felt how cold his lips were. "Are you cold, baby?" I asked, alarmed.

"No, I just drank some iced water," he said, smiling. "Relax, honey. I'm going to be okay." He was getting his first round of chemo.

I knew he would be okay today. But tomorrow, he would have an upset stomach and diarrhea. I lay on the bed beside him after his treatment, and we talked and cuddled. "I love you, Steven," I whispered after he had fallen asleep.

I left to find his doctor because I wanted to ask him if he knew any reputable psychiatrists, or if there was a practice nearby. I did not like Dr. Sekou Thomas!

I made an appointment to see Dr. Long the following Wednesday. He had come highly recommended by Steven's doctor. I delayed getting my prescription for the Zoloft. I didn't like that Dr. Thomas didn't let me know what the side effects were. I didn't like that

I wasn't able to talk to him and get a response. I spoke, and he sat there listening and then cut me off to tell me about Zoloft!

I spent the night at the hospital with Steven, and his mom joined me around 6:30 in the evening. I slept in one recliner, and she slept in the other. Just as I expected, Steven was sick to the stomach and weak that day. I felt sorry for him, but there wasn't much that could be done. If he took a sip of ginger ale, he threw it up within thirty minutes. I just made sure he was comfortable and resting.

Mrs. Marshall and I decided to go for a walk to get some fresh air and get away from the hospital for a few minutes.

20

"HAVE YOU EVER REGRETTED that Steven and I didn't make you a grandmother?" I asked.

"I would be lying if I said I didn't want any grandkids, but I never felt regret about it. I'm blessed to have my son here with me this long. For that, I am more than grateful," she said, smiling. *I loved this lady so much!*

A few days later I went to see Dr. Long, I was sure I was going to be able to talk to him, much like I did with Dr. Verlonda. He would give me something mild, tell me the side effects, and assure me that everything was going to be just fine. I was twenty minutes early for the appointment. I was busy reading a magazine when I heard my name called. I closed it, put it back on the table, stood up, heading to the entry. There stood an Asian doctor! Who knew that Jerome Long would be an Asian man? I sure as heck didn't know that!

I walked down the hallway beside him, and he stepped aside to let me into his office. The only things on the wall were his six degrees. There were no family photos on his desk or anything to personalize it. I sat down across from him, and he logged onto his computer. "So, what can I do for you?" he asked.

"I—I suffer from depression and anxiety." He put his glasses on and began reading from his computer screen, his lips moving quickly. Every once in a while, he said, "Ah, huh!"

After several minutes of silence, he asked if I had been prescribed any medication for it. "I have Zoloft." *Well, I didn't have them exactly, the drugstore did since I hadn't picked them up yet!*
"Okay, okay, I see that. You didn't like the Zoloft?"

"No," I said.

"Okay, I'm going to prescribe Celexa, 40 mg, and Trazodone. The instructions will be on the labels. Take the Celexa in the morning and the Trazodone at night. It will help with sleep, okay. Any questions?" he asked and stood up. I looked up at the clock on his wall. I had been in his office for eleven minutes!

"Yes, what are the side effects of these medications? And are they narcotics?" I asked.

He sat back down and picked up his pen. "Celexa causes a decrease in your sex drive. However, that will not be a problem for you. Women don't have any interest in sex anyway. My wife's favorite line each night is, 'I have a headache!' If you were a man, I would tell you it would cause erection problems or ejaculation problems. But, as I said, you women already have low libidos. The Trazodone may cause you drowsiness. Anything else?"

"These medications for depression and anxiety have so many side effects. So, I was wondering if you might know of any Chinese herbs or teas that can help me?" "Why're you asking me that? Because I'm Chinese? Are you asking me that because I'm Chinese?" he asked, now angry. He stood up, and so did I this time. I was finished here!

As I waited for the elevator, I couldn't help but laugh! Someone was playing a cruel joke on me! I honestly thought all of those shows that use to come on where they show the patient lying on the sofa, the shrink sitting in a chair nearby, listening intently, and taking notes were correct. No! They didn't want to hear my problems; all they wanted to do was give me a doggone prescription without any regard for the damage this mess would do to my body. So, he was going to prescribe something to help with my anxiety. However, it causes thoughts of suicide or rage against others, severe headaches, diarrhea, nausea, heart attack, tremors, seizures, and possibly death! There had to be something less traumatic than this crap!

I needed to get my hands on the *Back to Eden* book that my Daddy used to use back in the day.

"Daddy, do you still have that book *Back to Eden*?" I asked when he answered the phone.

"Yeah, it's my second Bible!"

"When you come to the hospital today, can you let me borrow it? Bring it when you come to the hospital, please."

I walked into Steven's hospital room; the bed was empty and stripped of sheets. Neither he nor his mom was anywhere to be seen. I panicked and rushed to the nurses' station. "Where is Steven Marshall?" I asked loudly.

"Calm down, baby. He was moved to room 411," she said and came around from the station to escort me there.

Steven was sleeping, and his mom was no longer there. I decided to text them, so they knew when they came to visit, he had been moved to another room, and they wouldn't panic as I did.

I sat there, staring out the window and thinking about the comical scene that just played out at Dr. Long's office. I got so tickled thinking about it that I had to laugh! I decided to stick with Dr. Verlonda and get those scenes on TV about the psychiatrist out of my head because apparently, they were not accurate.

While Steven slept, I thought about our lives together. I wished we had known about sterility before he had started the chemo. I would have loved to have a baby with my husband. Now, we would never know the joy of parenthood together.

21

I SAT IN A COFFEE SHOP, JUST around the corner from the hospital two weeks later, drinking coffee and eating a bagel when a man walked by. We made eye contact; he smiled and waved. I glanced around me to see if he were waving at me, or someone behind me. He pointed his finger at me, so I smiled.

He came into the shop and ordered a coffee and a sausage and egg on a roll. He stepped out of the line, he came to the table where I sat and said hello. I looked surprised because no one in New York had ever done that to me.

"Hello," I replied.

He held out his hand and introduced himself. "I'm Edgar Cowell."

I shook his hand. "Benita Marshall," I said, still surprised.

"I just wanted to say hi, Benita. I've seen you here before and thought to myself, the next time I see her, I was going to introduce myself."
He got his order, waved at the door, and left.

I watched as he went to the corner and waited to cross the street. The light changed, he looked back at me, caught me watching, and smiled again. I turned away, embarrassed.

After I had eaten, I went to the hospital to sit with Steven. He was awake and trying to eat his breakfast when I arrived. I kissed him on the cheek and checked out what he was eating.

"Is it good?" I asked. He looked at me sideways. "You should have called me; I could have gotten you something to eat."

He had received some fresh flowers and some new cards. I read them to him while he tried to eat his runny oatmeal and hard-boiled eggs.

At one, he had another chemo treatment scheduled, so I only sat with him for a few minutes and left to get my lunch from a nearby Chinese restaurant. Just as I was about to step into the elevator, Edgar Cowell was stepping off. He held the door for me, "Well, we meet again," he said. I smiled and entered the elevator.

I wondered what he was doing at the cancer center? Was he a doctor? Was he getting treatments or here to see a family member? I had to agree it was strange that we met again.

I returned with my lunch to find Steven laid back in the recliner with his eyes closed. "Are you sleeping?" I asked softly.

"No, just thinking." I saw he had been crying. I gently kissed him on the lips.

"Everything is going to be okay."

"I'm tired." He took my hand and kissed it. "I love you; I do. But I'm tired now."

"No, don't talk like that. We have our whole lives left."

"No, we don't. I think I'm going to stop the chemo."

"Steven, why? The doctors are hopeful that they can get it back in remission," I tried to reason.

"For how long? You don't think I see the pain in your eyes; my parent's eyes? You are so beautiful, and you deserve something more than what I can offer you. Please, let me talk," he said. I sat down and listened. "We've had some good times together, haven't we? I'm not afraid of dying, Bennie." I wiped the tears from his face. *Breathe! Breathe! Breathe!*

I was no longer hungry. I just wanted to hold my husband in my arms. I moved my chair closer to him and put my arms around him. We sat there just loving one another. I was heartbroken, but what could I do to convince him to live that I hadn't already done?

When he fell asleep, I went down the hall, carrying my takeout order, hoping I could find a microwave. One of the nurses warmed it up for me, and I went to the family lounge to eat. Thankfully, there was no one in there; I could be alone and try to pray again.

A few bites later, I realized I had lost my appetite. I closed the container and sat there, thinking about what my husband had said. I loved him very much, and I didn't want to lose him. I started crying. The more I thought about it, the more I cried. I was tired of bad news. *Breathe! Bennie, just breathe!*

I was crying hard; I didn't hear the door open, and someone come into the lounge.

"Is everything okay?" I heard a voice ask, and felt someone touching my shoulder. I looked up to see for the third time, Edgar Cowell. I reached in my lap for my napkin and wiped my eyes.

"No, everything is not okay. It's not okay," I cried. He pulled a chair up and sat in front of me.
"Do you want to talk about it?" he asked.
"My husband has leukemia, and he doesn't want to live anymore. He's tired! And I can't imagine my life without him in it," I cried.

"I'm sorry to hear that. I know how you feel." The way he said it, the tone of his voice let me know he might just know how I felt. I looked at him and saw he looked different from the other times I had seen him. There was a sadness about him.

"Are you a doctor?"
"No, I'm not a doctor. I was here with my mother. She passed away a little while ago." I felt horrible!

"I'm so sorry. Look at me crying and stuff, and you just lost your mother," I apologized.

"It's okay. My sisters and I made peace with the inevitable. She suffered for a long time. She's no longer in pain."

He started telling me about his mother. She was diagnosed with breast cancer and had a double mastectomy three years ago. After chemo and radiation, they thought they had gotten it all. But a year ago, it came back, this time in her brain, lungs, and liver. His hands were trembling, though his voice was steady. He reached into his jacket and removed his wallet. He pulled out a photo of his mother. "See, look. She's beautiful," he said, smiling.

I took the photo and agreed that she was beautiful. Edgar put it back into his wallet and closed it. "I have to be strong for my sisters. But enough about me; tell me about your husband."

"We've been married twenty-four years. He was diagnosed with leukemia when he was in high school. The doctors have been able to get it into remission twice, but now he's tired."

"I know you love him, but do you love him enough to let him go? We don't know the pain they feel. So, it would be selfish to want anything else for them, you understand me?" I knew what he meant.

I thanked him for taking the time to talk to me. I appreciated it. "All will be well," he said before leaving the room. I felt a little better after talking to him.

I called Daddy to tell him that Steven had decided he didn't want to go through any more chemotherapy. "So, what does that mean? Is he giving up?" Daddy asked.

"He's not giving up, Daddy. He's tired of being sick. He's just tired," I said. I knew he understood because Mommy had said the same thing before she passed away.

"I'll be over there in a little while." Daddy heard in my voice that I needed him with me. I got a cup of coffee from the vending machine and returned to the family lounge. Again, I was all alone, and this allowed me to pray.

After I said, "Dear Father," I choked up. I couldn't continue. I closed my eyes and asked God to read my heart. It was so heavy that my lips could not formulate the words I wanted to say.

My chest tightened up; I felt like I was going to have a heart attack. I tried to stand up, but my legs wouldn't move, and I couldn't catch my breath. *Breathe! Please, help me, Lord! Just Breathe! One, two, three! One, two, three! One, two! One, two!*

"Mrs. Marshall, are you okay?" Millicent, one of my

husband's nurses, asked me. I was sweating and gasping for air. I could only nod. She ran to the door and yelled for help.

It was just a panic attack, of course, but it was the worst one I had experienced thus far. I had to get it together so I could be strong for my husband and his family. I slid off the gurney, put my shoes on, and returned to my husband's bedside.

"I'm going home tomorrow," Steven said with a smile.

22

HOW WAS I EXPECTED TO WAIT for my husband to die? Who is the person that prepares one for such a traumatic event? Is there a program for something like that? What about a support group? What about a pill to help ease the pain?

I pulled out the sofa sleeper in the living room, moved the end table so that we could have room for Steven's IV machine and the portable toilet Hospice provided us.

Steven used to weigh 180 pounds but was down to about 130. He had lost his hair in patches. But once we got home, he asked me to shave his head. I had to put extra pillows on the sofa so that he could be comfortable.

"You don't have to sleep out here with me; I'll be okay," he said the first night. But I wanted to be near him; I wanted to make sure he was comfortable *and* alive.

I slept on the chaise part of the sofa, or rather I lay on the chaise. We watched old VHS movies, sipped tea, and looked at photo albums of the past twenty-plus years we had been together. Sometimes I laughed with him, honestly laughed, and sometimes I forced myself to laugh when all I wanted to do was cry.

I dozed off but woke up to see him watching me sleeping.

He had lost his appetite, but I was able to get him to eat a little applesauce or vegetable broth. I went online and researched ways to fight cancer. Daddy stayed with him while I went to the grocery store and ran other errands. I purchased fruits and vegetables that were alkaline and made smoothies, encouraging Steven to sip a little. I thought if he would drink them, he could be cured. Some days he would be upbeat, and on other days, he would be tired and listless.

His mother would go to the restroom and cry, and we sometimes heard her in the living room. But she always walked out composed. His dad was also trying to find a cure online and reading most of the same things I was reading.

Four months later, the nurse from Hospice came to visit and felt the doctor should be called in. I was so nervous that I could not think straight. The doctor finally arrived to examine Steven, I knew before he told me that my husband could not go on much longer. He hadn't eaten in four days. He had to be catheterized to urinate. His breathing was laborious, and he made gurgling sounds when he breathed. Each time the noises stopped, I tiptoed to him, gently held my hand on his chest to see if he was still breathing.

Steven's mom and I sat in the kitchen, holding hands and praying until the doctor completed his exam. He came in and pulled out a chair.

"I don't think he will make it through the day. We've increased his morphine drip to help make him comfortable. You might want to call the rest of the family over. I am sorry," he said. He hugged Mrs. Marshall and me and returned to the living room. He and the nurse whispered, and he left.

I pulled a stool close to the sofa bed and lay Steven's hand in my mine. It was so frigid. I leaned close to his ear and told him how much I loved him. "With all of my heart and soul, I love you, Steven." His eyelids fluttered as if he were trying to open them, and tears rolled down his face.

Two nights before, he had awakened me by tapping

on the wall. "I want you to promise me you will find someone else to love. I don't want you to be alone. Have a baby," he said in a hoarse voice.

I kept shaking my head. "Promise, promise," he said, looking deeply into my eyes.

"I don't know if I can. You were the best. I can't imagine my life without you. I don't know, Steven," I cried.

"Promise, please!"

"I promise," I finally said.

Steven took a deep gasping breath and never one after that. I looked at the nurse who was sitting nearby. She put the stethoscope against his chest and listened. She took his pulse, then turned to me and nodded.

"No! No!" I cried. Mrs. Marshall put her arms around me, and we cried together.

An ambulance arrived, and they confirmed what we

already knew. Steven was no longer breathing. I kissed his cold lips and let them carry him away.

I took the sheets off the sofa bed and closed it up. I rearranged the room the way it had been before letting out the bed four months ago. The nurse took the IV machine, the rest of her equipment, and left.

I called my daddy to come back because I needed him. I made the phone calls to Steven's father and his brothers. I called his job, and within two hours, our apartment was full of people from both of our families, his friends, frat brothers, and coworkers.

I looked around at all of those people and knew I had better get some food in the house. I ordered food from the Jamaican restaurant, the fish and chip joint, and the soul food restaurant. I went across the street to the store and purchased wine, sodas, and bottles of tea. I put the food on the dining room table, buffet style. I set up the drinks in the sink with ice and put out glasses for our guests.

I called everyone to come and get something to eat. I helped by making plates, pouring drinks, and making sure our guests were taken care of. *Breathe! One, two, three! One, two! One, two! One, two! One!*

Everyone was busy eating, talking, and telling stories about Steven and happy times, I retreated to my bedroom and lay on the bed crying. How was I going to go on? What was I going to go on for? What was left? I had loved this man for twenty-six years. I was his wife for twenty-four years, and now he was gone! I was all alone!

Promise me you won't cry for me. We had some great times together. Remember those times. Promise me. Promise me!" I had promised him that. I got up, entered the bathroom and washed my face. I fixed my hair and put on some lipstick. I changed into a dress and slipped on some shoes.

I returned to the living room. Someone had turned on the stereo, and jazz was playing in the background. I removed the empty containers from the dining table and made a salad. I was busying myself with making sure everyone was okay.

One of my neighbors had come over with fried chicken and baked ham. I put the chicken in the oven to warm up, cut the ham into slices, and placed on a tray. People kept asking me if I were okay. I smiled and said, "No, but I will be soon." I gratefully accepted their hugs and kisses on the cheek.

I walked guests to the door and kissed and hugged folk goodbye and thanked them for coming. By midnight, everyone had left except the immediate family. Steven's brothers and their wives left, going out when their parents did.

Daddy, CeeCee, and Trina were going to stay over with me. I appreciated that because there was no way I could be alone that night. Daddy and Trina cleaned up the kitchen and put the food away. Finally, around three, we went to bed. I sat up watching TV while Trina sat beside me. Daddy was in the guestroom sleeping.

I stepped to the bar, fixed myself a glass of gin, and drank it standing right there. I got a blanket and lay down on the sofa to sleep, clutching the pillow that Steven had laid on.

Again. I tried to pray to God. But I was so drunk that I couldn't get my words together.

The clock alarm sounded at eight that morning. I got up, took a hot shower, and got dressed. People would probably be coming by again today, so I went to the store again and got groceries. I cut up and seasoned several chickens and placed them in the refrigerator to marinate in buttermilk. I started making breakfast.

I was going to have to contact a funeral home and get a coffin, suit, and communicate with the insurance company and, and...and....and... *Breathe!*

The Marshalls, Daddy, and I were meeting with the funeral home director. He had gone to pick up Steven's body from the morgue. We were looking at coffins. I had taken the clothes Steven had wanted to be buried in with us to the funeral home. I kept telling myself I had to be strong for his mother. Every day for the three days before laying my husband to rest, my apartment was full of family, friends, Steven's frat brothers, and his parents.

The day of the funeral came and passed in a blur. I had to keep reminding myself to breathe that entire day. The funeral and graveside services were over, we went back to my apartment. That evening people dropped by, ate, and spent time with the family.

The door finally closed on the last guest, and I was relieved. I remembered how it was when my mother died. People quickly went back to their own lives after the funeral, leaving the family to fend for themselves. All of those, "I'll call you tomorrows, and call me if you need to talk" were well-meaning statements, but no one followed up on them.

"Daddy, I'm going to be okay. If not, I will catch a cab and come over to your house. But I am tired; I just want to get some rest."
"Are you sure?"
"Yes, I'm sure."

I leaned against the door of my now empty apartment. This was the beginning of my new life. I poured myself some gin in a shot glass and chugged it. I thought I would be okay with just one shot of gin. Nope! I put the shot glass on the bar and took the bottle with me.

I turned on the stereo and put in eight CDs with music from the 80s and began cleaning my apartment. In between the cleaning, I took a swig of gin. By four a.m., I was drunk as Cootie Brown, and could no longer go on. I lay down again and held Steven's pillow against my chest, inhaling his scent. I could not believe he was gone, and I was all alone. I could not wrap my mind around that, and I cried myself to sleep.

It became a pattern for me. I no longer slept in our bedroom, but on the sofa, clutching his pillow, drunk, and wallowing in pity.

I talked on the phone with family members whenever they called and tried to sound upbeat and normal. Inside, I was a mess! I had a refrigerator full of spoiled food. Three weeks after the funeral, I went on another cleaning spree and threw out all the food in the fridge.

I wrote out checks to pay some bills, went to the grocery store, and dropped them all off in the mailbox on the corner.

I walked home slowly, pulling the shopping cart behind me. I was crossing the street, looking straight ahead when I heard someone call my name. I looked up, and it was Edgar.

"How are you doing? How's it going? It's been a while," he said, smiling.

I removed the headphone from my ear. "It's been okay. I'm okay."

He came across the street with me, and we stood on the corner, talking. "How is your husband?"

"He passed away about a month ago."

"I'm sorry to hear that. How are you doing?" he asked again.

"I'm okay."

"Do you live around here?"

"Yes, I do. I have to go. It was good seeing you."

"Here, let me give you my card. If you ever feel like talking, call me." He held out his hand, and I took the card. I thanked him and went home.

I put up the food I had purchased and made myself a burger and salad for lunch. I poured some Beefeater's over a glass of ice and filled it the rest of the way with orange juice. I ate and cried. I was a mess, and this was not what Steven would have wanted. I took a shower and fixed myself up and decided to visit Trina.

"Hey, Trina, are you busy?" I asked when she answered the phone.

"No, what's up?"

"Would you like to go to the city, walk around in Times Square, go to Harlem? I have to get out of this apartment."

"Sure, I'll be there around two."

"No, I can come and get you. We can drive," I said.

I hadn't taken the car out since before Steven had come home from the hospital. I got to Trina's building, called to let her know I was downstairs and to come on down. Instead of going to Times Square, we went to Harlem for an early dinner.

I didn't realize this was Steven's and my favorite restaurant until Trina and I were nearly finished with our meal. We loved eating breakfast at Amy Ruth's on Sunday mornings. *Breathe!*

I forced myself to smile and enjoy the meal with my sister. I let her know I was proud of her. She smiled and reached for my hand. "I have a great example to follow."

I ordered us a plate to go, a red velvet cake, and we headed back to Brooklyn. On the way there, Trina offered to spend the night if I wanted company. I assured her I was okay and thanked her.

Once I got back inside my apartment, the feeling of despair tried to take over. I had to shake that feeling! I fixed myself a drink, turned on the TV, and began eating a slice of red velvet cake. It was good. I wanted some more, so I ate a second slice. While I was in the kitchen, I got the Hellavugood French onion dip and a bag of Ruffles' potato chips. I pigged out all night long and drank myself into a stupor.

The next morning, I felt horrible. I spent most of the morning in the bathroom, sick to the stomach with diarrhea. Out of curiosity, I stepped on the scale. I was shocked when it said 160 pounds. There was no way I was going to be fat and depressed. I pulled on my sweatsuit and headed to the gym.

I was running on the treadmill and sipping my gin and juice. I looked up and saw Edgar working out on the weights. I hoped he wouldn't see me. I just wanted to be left alone!

I was able to complete my work-out and get out of there without being bothered. At home, I took a warm shower and shampooed my hair. While I was applying oil to my body, it occurred to me that I had not been made love to in almost two years.

I got dressed in one of Steven's shirts and drank myself into another drunken mess.

23

"I NEED TO MAKE AN APPOINTMENT to see one of your doctors," I said to the receptionist on the phone at the psychiatrist's office I found in the yellow pages. I hoped I would have better success with someone at their practice than the last psychiatrist's office.

I also made an appointment to start seeing my therapist again.

We were coming up on a year since he had passed. I hadn't returned to work. I spent my days drinking from the time I awakened to the time I went to bed and even got up in the middle of the night to get a refill. If I wasn't drinking, I was putting on a good front for my family.

It was good seeing her after all of this time. I'm sure it had been a year since our last visit.

"How have you been, Benita? You look great," she said.

"I'm not doing well," I replied honestly.

"I know Steven would be very disappointed in me because I had prepared myself for his passing. I had even promised him that I would not mourn like this, and I would give love another chance. I also promised I would marry again and have a baby."

"Have you cleared out his closets, put away his things, donated them, or whatever?"

"No. I haven't. I keep wanting to, but I stop myself; it's like if his things are still in the closets, I feel he is still there."

"But he is not there, sweetie. You have to let his things go so that you can move on. As long as you hold on to them, do you think you are ever going to be able to go on?" She was right. I had to move on now.

I decided to call his brothers and see if they would come over and look through Steven's things to see if there was anything they wanted to keep. If not, we were going to donate them to a halfway house that allowed former inmates to get back on their feet.

His brothers loaded up their car with Steven's things. I waved goodbye to them. I went back upstairs, I felt a different air in the room. I felt a bit free. I cleaned up the apartment, rearranged the furniture, put up different curtains, and took down art I had only gotten because Steven liked it. I wasn't trying to erase him from my life; I just wanted to move on.

Steven had two insurance policies. I put one into a savings account and lived off of the other for the past year. I also had his 401K that had been transferred into my savings. I could have stayed home five years or so, but I decided I wanted to get back to work.

Monday morning, I was on the subway heading to my old job to see if I could get it back. I took family medical leave, and when that was up, I decided to resign. My supervisor informed me that I could come back anytime I wanted, so I was going to start there first.

"I am so glad you returned. We would love to have you back. When do you think you can start?" she asked.

I said, "I could be available to start the next Monday."

I was going to try and start the next day, but I was panicking. I didn't even know if I were ready to start back.

Before going up to my apartment, I stopped and got myself an Italian sub, and then went home. I let myself in and kicked off my shoes. "I got my job back!" I said out loud. I wished Steven could have heard me, but ... *Breathe!*

I changed clothes and fixed a drink. It was after midnight when I finally woke up. I put on my pajamas and fixed another drink. I went to my bedroom, clutching a bottle of Beefeater's Gin, I fell across the bed crying. I was lonely! I didn't want to be alone!

I cried so much that night, when I woke up, my head was killing me. I made a pot of coffee and called Daddy. "Hey, baby. Whatcha doing today?" he asked.
I wasn't doing anything and hoped he was so I could get out of this apartment.

"I was going to the VA and check on some business and maybe have lunch at Woo Hop. Do you want to come? Get out of the house," he said.

While I was getting ready to go with Daddy, I looked

at my reflection in the mirror. I looked a hot mess. I hadn't shampooed my hair in at least three months. It was matted and funky. My lips were chapped and cracked. I got in the shower and let the water beat down on me while I cried. I shampooed my hair and spent nearly ½ hour trying to get it combed out so I could put it in two big braids. I got dressed, put on makeup to hide the bags under my eyes, and sported sunglasses to hide my bloodshot eyes.

I sat outside to wait for Daddy to come, hoping the fresh air would rejuvenate me. It didn't!

24

BEING WITH MY DAD ALWAYS made me feel better, and I wished I could tell him what I was going through. I knew deep down he would have been able to help me because he had gone through the same thing when Mommy passed away. But I couldn't bring myself to do it. I wanted my misery all to myself. I was ashamed, too. I was ashamed I had turned to alcohol to drown my sorrow. I was a mess!

Later, as we sat in the Chinese restaurant, I was tempted to say something to Daddy about this burden I was carrying, but he was in such a good mood, and I didn't want to bring him down. I placed a smile on my face and played the role I thought was expected of me.

DARBY WEST

As the days zoomed by and Sunday night rolled around, there was no way I was going to be able to go to work on Monday morning. I just wasn't ready. I cried all night Sunday night. Early Monday morning, I called my supervisor's office. Knowing she wasn't in yet, I left her a voicemail. I apologized and said I couldn't come in. I didn't know when I was going to be able to come back, but I appreciated her for giving me another chance. I hung up and got drunk. Each time I sobered up, I got drunk again.

Later that morning, I thought my therapist was in and called her office. She answered, and all I could do was break down crying.

She asked, "Why don't you come right over?"
I slipped on a pair of sweatpants, a halter top, and took the bus to her office. I didn't even think about combing my hair until I saw my reflection in the glass of her door. I looked horrible. I was embarrassed. No wonder people on the bus were

staring at me like I was crazy.

I had cried for a good fifteen minutes before I was able to calm down enough to tell her that I was falling apart. "I just want to die! I don't have anything to live for. I'm tired!"

"Have you thought about hurting yourself?"
Every time I poured a glass of gin, I wanted to die.
She leaned forward, looked me in the face, and asked, "Do you want to go to the hospital for a few days. You can sign yourself in and leave when you think you are ready. I believe you need to do that, Benita."
She wanted to do it right then; just call an ambulance, and they would take me straight to the hospital. I said, "I want to let my dad and the Marshalls know first."
"I will call them for you," she responded.

If I were to go, it was going to have to be by my

rules. I wasn't going anywhere in an ambulance, and I had to let my family know first. I promised her that I would go that day and have the hospital call her when I got there. I needed to take a shower. I rushed out of her office and took the bus home.

I packed a bag with some sweats and t-shirts, underwear, and bras. I took a hot shower, put my hair in three braids, and wrapped it in African fabric. I locked up my apartment and called a taxi to take me to Mount Sinai Hospital. I cried all the way there. *Breathe! One, two, three! One, two, three! One, two!*

25

I PAID MY FARE AND STEPPED out of the taxi, carrying my overnight bag. I walked into the ER, shaking, sweating, and crying.

"My name is Benita Marshall, and I came here because I am afraid I might commit suicide tonight," I said through tears. The nurse stood up and came around to get me. She led me to an intake room and asked me to sit down. She told the nurse there I needed to be seen right away.

I repeated my name and gave my address while another nurse began taking my blood pressure and temperature. Placed in a wheelchair, another nurse wheeled me to the psych ward. Finally, I was rolled in front of another nurse; she stood and came around the counter. Both of them helped me out of the wheelchair. She took me to a small room about as big as a cell. There was a TV mounted high on the wall, showing the news. She opened my bag and removed each of my items of clothing, shook it, and folded it back up.

I lay down on the cot and pulled the blanket over me. Freezing, I asked for another blanket. One of the nurses left the room and returned a few minutes later with a warm blanket. He placed it over me and patted my shoulder. "We are going to get you a room ready, okay. Just try to relax. If you need anything, the buzzer is right behind you on the wall. Just press it if you need me," he said softly and left the room, closing the door behind him.

As soon as he left, I remembered I hadn't called my dad. I eased out of the cot and opened the door. "Can you please call my father?" I asked.

"Sure, honey." I gave him the phone number and lay

back down, pulling the covers around my neck.

As I lay there, I thought about the promises I had broken with Steven. I felt horrible and began crying. There was a box of tissue on the table beneath the TV. I got up to get the box and noticed a camera in the corner of the wall. When I lay back down, I wondered if I was being watched. I didn't even care!

I eventually went to sleep only to be awakened by the nurse again. "Wake up, honey, we have your room ready," he said. I looked at his badge and saw it said Bruce G.
He helped me up, and I sat in the wheelchair. I was wheeled to the elevator, holding my bag in my lap as we got into it.

we stepped off the elevator on the ninth floor, Bruce wheeled me to another nurses' station. A nurse named Lisa M. stood and came around to me. She introduced herself as Ms. Morrow and said she was training a young lady named Millicent. The two of them were going to get me checked into their ward. They helped me to a well-lit room, where there was a toilet with a shower. I sat down in the chair they pointed to, and they began the checking in process with me.

"I'm going to need you to undress and put this gown on," Ms. Morrow said. I went to the bathroom, but there was no door. "Don't worry; we have the same thing," she told me.

I turned my back and removed my clothing. I took the gown off the hook and started to put it on. "Before you put it on, I need to do a body search. I'm just going to pat you down; I'm not going to do a cavity check, okay."

She touched my breast and down the front and back of my panties. Satisfied that I had no pills, guns, or other harmful items, she let me put on the gown.

She tied it on the side for me and gave me another one to put on that tied in the front.

"I'm going to need you to remove the scarf," she said. I pulled it off and handed it to her. My long braids fell around my shoulders. She squeezed my braids to make sure I didn't have a weapon in them.

We went back to the nurses' station, and she said, "Have a seat by the wall," while she got her equipment. Upon return, she took my vital signs. "The doctor on-call has prescribed 20mg of Celexa and 10mg of Melatonin to help you get to sleep."

She gave me the meds in a small cup and handed me a paper cup of water. I swallowed them quickly and gave her the cups. "Open your mouth, please," she ordered. I opened my mouth, and she looked inside.

She smiled and patted me on the shoulder. "Come

on; we'll take you to your room," she said, leading me down the hallway. I glanced at the clock on the way and was shocked to see it was after ten p.m. Where had the day gone?

There was a woman in a hospital bed on one side of the room. She had a small light on above her bed and turned to see what the commotion was when we entered. "Go back to sleep, Sara," Ms. Morrow said. Sara mumbled something, but I couldn't make out what it was.

Ms. Morrow showed me the empty cot that was a plastic covered mattress resting on a wooden platform. The blankets were folded at the foot of the bed; there was one flat pillow to rest my head on.

I lay down, and Ms. Morrow pulled the covers over me. "Are you warm enough? This seems to be the coldest room on the floor," she said. I asked for two more blankets and a better pillow.

I was crying again when she returned with the blankets and pillow. She covered me with them and asked me if I were okay. "No, but I will be," I said.

"I want you to know that we make safety rounds every fifteen minutes. We will just open the door and peek in. If you are awake, say hello or something to let us know you are not sleeping because we have to keep an accurate log of your sleeping habits, okay," she said. I thanked her and turned over to face the wall. I had never liked to take medicine, and as the room began spinning, I was not going to be able to take that Celexa.

Breathe, Bennie! One, two! One, two! One!

At three in the morning, I got up because my legs were cramping. I wobbled to the nurses' station and asked for Ms. Morrow. I was informed she had gone for the night, and the replacement nurse was helping another patient. There was a large room right off from the nurses' station that had a seating area and dining tables near the window. I sat down in one of the chairs and waited for the new nurse to return. My legs were hurting so badly it felt as if they had been beaten with a bat.

By the time she returned, I was nearly in tears. "Hi, Benita. I'm Ramona. What's going on?" she asked.

I said, "My legs are hurting really bad."

"Let me let the doctor know, and I'll be right back."

She returned and gave me some warm compresses. I didn't care what she got for my pain; I would have accepted it. *Breathe!* I wished I had some Beefeaters!

She wrapped the warm damp towels around my legs and elevated them by placing my feet on a chair. She came back again, this time she had some medicine in a cup and a small paper cup of water. "I have some Tylenol for you. After you take them, why don't you go back to bed and try to get some rest?

You'll feel so much better in the morning."

"Thank you, Ms. Ramona."

"You're welcome, sweetie. If you need anything, just press the buzzer."

I cried myself to sleep that night just as I had done every night since Steven passed away. The only difference was this night, I did not have any liquor to help me get to sleep. I tossed, turned, and cried all night long. It kept my roommate up, so I was moved to a private room. I had a choice to sleep in the standard hospital bed, or on the cot. I chose a hospital bed. It had to be more comfortable than lying on that plastic contraption.

Being alone was much better. I was also given another Melatonin. This time, I went to sleep. But before I could get into it, a loud-mouth nurse came in, calling me to get up and come get my vitals because it was almost time for breakfast. I got up and went to the bathroom. The mirror was a rectangle piece of tin, instead of glass. My reflection was distorted and matched the exact way I was feeling. I washed my face and used the bathroom. The same woman came in, calling me again. "Okay, I'm coming!" I said.

I quickly finished washing my hands and went to the "community room."

I was surprised to see men there. I thought they would be in a separate area. Everyone was lined up, waiting to get their vital signs checked. While I was in line, a commotion was going on behind me.

"Get back here! Where do you think you're going? Don't start this crap today! Someone yelled. I turned to see what was going on. A young Chinese woman was attempting to leave out of the employee entrance when the employee came in with the food cart.

A security officer was trying to prevent her exit by standing in front of the door. A male nurse was gently pushing her away. I couldn't tell if the woman was speaking Chinese or English because she was talking fast.

"She does these breaks for it fifty times a day," the man behind me said. I turned back around and tried to tune it all out. I just wanted to get my vital signs taken so I could return to my room. I saw from where I was standing what some of the patients were eating, and it didn't look appealing.

At my turn, I sat down and rolled up my sleeve. "Good morning. You're new, huh?" the nurse asked.

"Yes," I said.

"I'm Monnie, but everyone calls me Momma. I don't force anyone to do that. So, you can call me whatever you want to call me. I will answer to either of them."

"I'm Benita Marshall." She checked my armband and entered something into the laptop she was using.

After taking my vitals, she gave me a cup with a pill in it. "What is this?"

"This is your Celexa."

"Can you see if the doctor got back with the other nurse because the Celexa was giving me cramps in my legs?"

"The doctor said that you will experience cramps until your body adjusts," she said, thrusting the cup in my direction again. I didn't want to take this medication.

"Please, take your medication! Don't you want to feel better?"

I wasn't making any headway with this woman, so I took the cup and swallowed the Celexa. As I was going up the hall back to my room, another nurse called my name. I went to see what she wanted, and she handed me a tray of food.

I took the tray and went to sit at an empty table. I had a banana, a cup of strawberry yogurt, a cold bagel, and two boiled eggs. That was the standard breakfast if you didn't order one.

We were each given the menus for the next two meals. I looked over it and decided to get the burger and fries for lunch and the baked chicken and broccoli for dinner.

After I had eaten my banana and yogurt, I took the tray back and went to bed.

I was shaking and sweating and knew it was withdrawals from the alcohol. I pulled the cover around my neck and tried to keep my teeth from chattering.

Ms. Marcia came in to check on me. She pulled a chair beside my bed. "Tell me what is going on with you? Were you using narcotics?" she asked.

"No, I was...I drank a half-gallon of gin every day for the past year," I responded, shivering.

"The doctors are doing rounds. When they come

around, I will tell him, okay. In the meantime, would you like some tea or coffee?"

"I would like some gin!"

She patted me on the shoulder and said, "Try to relax, dear."

By the time the doctors arrived, I was a mess! I wasn't cold, but I could not stop shaking. One of the doctors introduced himself and said he would be taking care of me during my stay. He briefly introduced the interns with him.

He said he was going to prescribe Librium, and the nurse would bring it by. "We also have a psychiatrist coming by in about twenty minutes to speak with you. You sit tight, and she will be here in a moment with the medication."

I anxiously waited for the nurse to return with the medicine. I was in the bathroom hanging over the commode when she entered, dry heaving. My braids caught the bulk of the green bile I threw up. She held them out of the way while I gagged and heaved.

She helped me to get back into the bed and gave me the medication to take. "May I have some ginger ale?" I asked.

"Let me get this mess out of your hair first," she said. After she had got my braids cleaned off, she went to get my ginger ale.

The nurse also gave me a pan to regurgitate in. I needed my daddy! I could not believe I was in a psych ward at a hospital, throwing up and shivering from alcoholism! *One! One! One! One! One!*

I started crying, and this time, I wasn't sure how I would be able to stop or if I wanted to. I wanted to just die! *One! One! One! One! One! One! One! One! One! One! One!*

26

THE FIRST TWO DAYS AT THE facility were horrible. I never felt so badly before in my life! *Breathe!*

It wasn't enough I had to deal with my issues, but every five or ten minutes this crazy Chinese chick; Julie was racing toward the exits. I had no idea where Julie thought she was going because that doorway led to the service elevators, which meant she would only end up in the kitchen. As long as Julie was wearing a hospital gown, they would undoubtedly bring her crazy behind back to the psych ward. It didn't stop her, though.

On my third evening there, a schizophrenic patient arrived. I was sitting up in the community room, unable to sleep or get comfortable. When she was admitted, I was sitting in the semi-dark, thinking about how I had gotten to this place in my life. She arrived wearing a hospital gown. Her hair was long and matted, and cuts were healing on her legs.

She stared straight ahead with a blank expression, moving in slow motion. Her glasses were sideways on her face. Two nurses led her to the chair where our vital signs were taken, but she wasn't cooperating with them. Over and over, they told her that they had to take her vital signs.

"Please, give me your arm, Stella," they begged.
Finally, they called a male nurse over. He stood in front of the woman with his back turned; her arm stretched out in front of her. He held it in that position until they took her blood pressure. After they finished taking her vitals, they went down the hallway. I had this horrible feeling they were taking this woman to my room! I got up, looked down the hall to see where they were going. Yep! They walked

her into my room! I hurried down the hall. "Oh, hell, no! She ain't staying in here with me!" I shouted angrily. I was fine being in a room with a roommate. But not someone schizo! No way!

Both nurses turned to look at me, surprised by my outburst. After all, I had been sweet and quiet since I had gotten there. But I was not going to share a room with this woman!

"You don't have a choice," the male nurse said from behind me. Stella walked right over to my unmade bed and sat down. "No, Stella, someone already sleeps there. Your bed is over here," one of the nurses said.

She refused to get up! They tugged and tugged, but she was not budging. The male nurse went to help them. When they got her up, I noticed that her gown had come undone in the back, and this woman didn't have on panties.

"I need clean sheets now!" I said, totally pissed off about having her nasty, naked behind on my sheets! *One! One! One!*

"Lonnie, can you please take Ms. Bennie back to the community room!" Ms. Marcia said with an edge to her voice. He reached for my arm, but I snatched it away. I had to call my daddy! I hadn't seen him in three days, and though we talked a few times every day, I needed him to come and get me.

I picked up the phone, but it was turned off for the night. "Turn on the phone, please! Turn on the phone! I need to call my daddy to come and get me!" I shouted.

I am not a belligerent person, and I don't even know why I was tripping. But I was angry! The security guard came from behind the plate glass enclosure where the nurses' station was located and requested I calm down and go back to the community room. It was three in the morning; I was wide awake, wired, and ready to kick somebody's, anybody's behind! "Mind your business! Ain't nobody talking to you!" I said.

"Go and sit down, Bennie," he said calmly.

Lonnie was standing there to prevent me from going back down the hallway to my room. I got a glimpse of me in the reflection of the plate glass at the nurses' station. I looked again and was ashamed. I could not believe I was acting a fool like this! I started crying, stumbled into the community room, and sat down. It had to be a side effect of the medication they had given me. I had never raised my voice to anyone.

I was so loud I woke up the crazy Chinese chick, and here she came running toward the exit doors locked this time of night. Lonnie caught her just as she was running past him. He swung her around and led her back to her room. For the next two hours, that was the game that she, Lonnie, and the security guard played.

At five-thirty in the morning, Ms. Marcia came and sat in the chair beside me. "Are you doing okay?" she asked, sounding concerned.

"I apologize. I don't know what got into me. I don't want to be in the room with that woman, but I should not have yelled like that," I said calmly.

"You don't get to pick who you want to room with, sweetie. You know, we check on you all every fifteen minutes to make sure you are safe. Is that your concern?" "Yeah, that's one of them."

"She's not going to bother you," she assured me.

And the sky is pink. I stayed in the community room until I felt so tired that I could hardly stay awake. When I returned to my room, Stella's crazy behind was lying in my bed.

I marched right back to the nurse's station and told them what she was doing. "Go in the community room, while we get her up and get the bed changed again," Ms. Marcia said.

"Lonnie! Lonnie!" Ms. Marcia yelled. He went running down the hallway, followed by the security guard. I stood in the hallway, waiting to see what the heck was going on. I heard things being knocked over. Stella was screaming like a wild woman. One of the nurses at the nurses' station opened the door and said, "Go and sit down in the community room."

I listened this time because whatever was going on in my room was severe. Surely, they would put her in a separate room now. Maybe she even needed to be in a padded room clothed in a straightjacket.

Her screaming woke up the crazy Chinese chick, who came out of her room, saw everyone who could stop her was helping the woman in my room, so she made a mad dash for the door again. It was locked, of course, but it didn't stop her. She pushed her weight against it several times, and nothing happened. Well, let me rephrase that; her robe came undone in the back, and she stood there with her red panties showing, but the door remained locked. This was too much for me. I thought I was going to be able to get some much-needed therapy, rest, get my mind straight. There was way too much drama here! *Breathe! Breathe!*

They turned on the phones the next morning after breakfast, so, I called Daddy. I told him that I was ready to come home. "These folks are driving me crazy!" I whispered so no one heard me.

"You've only been there for four days. Have they even been able to help you yet? Come on, baby. Tune them folks out, and just do you," he said.

I sighed heavily and was about to hang up. Then, I said, "Please, come visit me. "I will do that."

"Today, Daddy," I added. *One! One! One!*

Stella was moved to another room that morning. I couldn't enter my room until it had been cleaned. I didn't look, but some of the other patients said she must have cut herself on something because there was blood all over the floor and walls. By the time I returned to take a shower, things were back to normal. I closed the door to my room to take a hot shower and was cautious about doing it because there were no locks on any of the doors; everyone was free to wander around if they wanted to. I didn't feel comfortable with the guys in the same ward as the women, but who was I to speak out about it.

I got a chance to speak with a psychiatrist and two interns after breakfast. I didn't know how to pronounce her Nigerian last name, but her first name was easy enough, Kim.

"I don't understand why the men are in the same ward as the women. You don't think it is dangerous?" I asked

"We do have two security guards. What do you think will happen?"

"You're joking, right? Did you see that little stunt that Julie pulled earlier? Her hospital gown was up around her waist! We all got to see her naked behind. It didn't turn me on, but what about if one of these guys got turned on?" I said. I could not believe I was having this conversation with this woman!

Again, she acted like having the men and women together was a good thing.

"Well, when can I go home?"

"I will discuss that with your doctor, and we will get back with you."

I wasn't ready to go home and knew it. When my session was over, I went to my room to try and get some sleep. I hadn't slept any the night before. It seemed things had calmed down in the ward, and I might be able to get some rest.

I did doze off to sleep and was sleeping well until I felt someone tugging at my sheets, and saying, "Get up! Get up!" I turned to see Stella had made her way back to my room and was trying to get me to get out of what she thought was her bed. I scrambled around, feeling for the buzzer to get the nurses. She wasn't doing anything to me physically, but I didn't know what she was capable of doing.

I knew I had better get out of that bed! *One! One! One! One! One! One!*
The nurses and the security guard came in and removed her from my room. I badly wanted a drink. *One! One! One! One! One!*

I ate a few French fries at lunchtime and put my tray up. "You have to start eating. That's not good for you," the assistant said. I just didn't have an appetite. I was tired and had begun shaking again with chills. I asked for another blanket and was about to go to my room when my dad showed up. I was glad to see him!

We couldn't sit at the table because people were still eating; we sat in the community room chairs.

"How are you doing, baby?" Daddy asked.

"I'm ready to go home," I lied.

"C'mon, girl. You know you're not ready to go home yet. I think you should ask if you can be transferred to a facility that will detox you from alcohol and get from around these folks. This is not where you need to be. Do you want me to speak with them?"

He was right. I needed to be in a facility for alcoholics, not a psych ward!

27

THREE DAYS LATER, I WAS on my way to the Unity Behavioral Health Center in Tampa, Florida. As soon as I walked into the building, I knew this was where I should be.

I didn't have to deal with crazy people running in the halls, trying to escape. Everyone there was there because they realized they needed help and were willing to get it.

I signed into the facility and was shown to my room. The facility was relatively new and still had the new smell to it. There were two beds in the room, not hospital beds, but regular beds with two chests and a TV. I didn't have a roommate at the time.

I checked in during a group session, so I was given a

tour of the facility. There was a movie theater. The dining room was very nice. I smelt the food the staff was preparing for lunch, and it smelled wonderful. I was ready to be happy again, and I was glad I was here.

I have to admit I got too excited. I don't know what I expected to be going on here, but it wasn't all sugar and cream. That afternoon at lunchtime, I went to the cafeteria where several patients were already eating or waiting in line. I got in the line behind a young white woman wearing a bright orange sundress.

I spoke to her; she turned to look at me and rolled her eyes. Then she turned around without responding. That was okay with me, but it didn't sit well with the older woman behind me. "Do you see how these little runts act now? They don't even have the decency to say hello when someone speaks to them," she said to me, but loud enough for the young woman to hear.

"Go to hell!" she said, looking at me, and I wasn't even the one who said something.

She and I reached for the tray at the same time. I thought she had a tray already because she kept walking past them. I lifted my hand and let her have the tray. It wasn't that big of a deal. Unfortunately, it irritated the woman behind me, and she scolded the young lady again.

I was wondering if there was anywhere I could go without folks acting a fool! "Leave me alone, Margaret!" the young lady shouted.

The old woman tried to draw me into the imaginary drama she was having with the young lady. "I just came for the food," I said. That shut that conversation down quickly.

I told the staff member what I wanted to eat, and

she put it in serving dishes for me and handed them to me. I made sure to thank her. I looked around for an empty table and went to sit down. To my surprise, the young woman came and sat at my table. I prayed I would not have to get drawn into any drama. I just wanted to eat my lunch and then go to my first meeting with my doctor. That was all!

"I'm Jennifer," she said after I lifted my head.
"I'm Benita. It's nice to meet you."
I sprinkled some salt on my mashed potatoes and salad and tasted my lasagna. "We have lasagna every Tuesday."
"It's really good!"

I was shocked, considering the slop I had to eat back at the hospital in New York.
"Yeah, they serve some great meals. It's just the people here that suck!"
She apologized for yelling at me.
"I thought you were that crazy, Natalie! She's had it

in for me ever since I got here."

"Did you all know each other before you came here?"

"Heck no! I ain't never seen that chick before! She's just mad cause she can't get a drink or something."

Our table had six empty seats, but soon, they were all taken. Everyone introduced themselves to me and was very helpful. I had been told before coming here that I was coming to get well, not to make friends, and I kept that in mind. I wasn't going to disrespect anyone, but I wasn't planning on giving out my contact information to anyone before I left here. I just let them all talk and kept my opinions to myself.

After lunch, I met with a counselor, and we discussed my plan of action. I was tired of being drunk and wanted to be sober. It was as simple as that. For more than thirty years, I had been turning to alcohol to cope with life's stresses. It was time to find a new way to manage.

I was expected to attend group meetings as often as they held them. I was supposed to interact with others and be respectful in those interactions. We had a movie night on Wednesday, Friday, and Saturday night. We picked a movie to watch from the list, and the movie with the most points was the one that was chosen. We were expected to be respectful of the staff and know that any infractions were punishable by removing privileges. I was cool with everything the counselor shared with me. I just wanted to get well; that was all!

In twenty-eight days, I was going to zoom through this program and learn how to be a sober person. I concentrated on that. I prayed and memorized the twelve steps.

However, I had a problem with the idea I was to forever refer to myself as an alcoholic. It seemed to me that if I completed rehab, stopped drinking, and learned to deal with my issues more productively, I was no longer an alcoholic. Since I didn't want to rock the boat, I kept my opinion to myself in the group and discussed it with my counselor.

He tried to explain it to me, and I saw his lips moving and the words coming out of his mouth, but to me, I just could not wrap my mind around that stigma. To me, being an alcoholic kept me in bondage. I was a slave to the bottle. If I were no longer drinking, I was free. Anyway, I decided to keep it to myself and not even share my thoughts regarding it with my counselor.

Twenty-eight days later, I was ret' to go!

I packed my suitcase and said goodbye to everyone. I wanted to smell the ocean air one more time; I stood on the pier and inhaled that fresh air. *I could breathe!*

28

I WAS HOME! I WAS HOME! The first thing I did was open the windows and let the fresh air flow into my space. It felt good to be home!

I was determined that come Monday morning, I was going to go looking for a job, so I needed to get to a salon to get something done to my hair. I changed clothes and headed to Hair Fashion East to get my hair done. I hadn't been to the salon in almost two years. I left there feeling like a princess. Nobody had to tell me I was looking good because I knew I was looking good!

I got on the train at 34th Street, who should I see at the other end of the car but Edgar Cowell. "Hello! Hello!" he said.

"You know if I didn't know better, I would think you are following me," I joked. "What can I say? How have you been doing?"

"I'm doing good, thanks. I'm doing good."

"You look great. Happy, different."

"Thank you," I said.

We talked on the way to our stop in Brooklyn. As we came up from the subway, he asked if we could meet sometime soon for coffee or drinks.

"Coffee sounds good," I said. He took out his cell phone and entered my phone number.

"You know what? I'm going to call you right now because I know how you ladies are. You give a brother just any old number. Hold up," he said.

He called me. I took my phone out and answered it.

"Hi Edgar," I said, laughing.

"Okay, so you're on the up and up! I'll see you tomorrow."

"Call me!" I said, and walked on home, smiling.

I called Trina to make plans with her and my niece to hang out on the weekend. While I was talking to her,

I got a call from Edgar.

"Girl, I will speak to you later," I said.

"How have you been doing since the last time I saw you? What, a year ago?"

"I had a rough time for a while. I kind of lost my way. I needed help finding it again. Now, I am better," I confessed.

"Yeah? Well, I'm glad you decided to get help. That's taboo in our community, you know."

"How have you and your sisters been doing since your mom's death?"

"You remember. We had it rough at first, too. But I thought about how much suffering my mother was going through, and I didn't want to see her living in that much pain. I feel her every day in some way. I think about the things she taught my sisters and me. We're okay. I miss her, but I'm okay."

It was good to talk to an adult who was not my

daddy or my sister. I missed the Marshalls because we had been like family for twenty-four years, but the relationship had changed. Not because I wanted it to, but because they seemed to not want me to be a part of their family anymore. I learned in counseling that it was okay for them to feel that way. Everyone is entitled to their feelings. Perhaps my presence held some memories that pained them. I hoped they would come around. If they didn't, I would give them their space.

The day Edgar and I were to meet for coffee, I stood in my closet, not knowing what to wear. I knew this wasn't a date, but it felt like one. And I had no clue what to wear on a date. I hadn't been on one in fitty-leven years. The only person I had ever dated was Steven, and we were kids when we started seeing each other. I went online and looked through Pinterest to get some ideas about what to wear. I finally decided on a pair of black skinny jeans, a white tank top, and a yellow jacket.

When Edgar called me to tell me he was downstairs and that I had never given him my apartment number, I wasn't sure if I wanted him to come up. *Breathe!*

"I live on the fourth floor, apartment 411," I said.

I went to the living room to make sure everything was neat and in order. He rang the bell, and I stepped to the side and let him in.

"Have a seat. I just have a couple more things to do, and I'll be ready,"

"You have a beautiful place. I like your decorating style. I love the African art," he said, going to the wall to look closer.

I left him there and went back to my bedroom to finish putting on my makeup.

I hated to admit it, but I only drank plain coffee. I didn't know what "grande" meant. I had never had a

Macchiato anything. I just drank plain old coffee! Edgar returned to the table, carrying a large glass of some type of coffee with lots of whipped cream, chocolate shavings, and a cherry on top. To me, that was more like a milkshake.

"Don't knock it until you've tried it!" he said, laughing. Then asked, "How did you meet your husband?"

"We went to the same high school. And one day, our English teacher paired us up to do a project together, and we were together ever since. We went to college in the same city. I went to Spellman, and he was at Morehouse. You've never been married?"

"I was married once. We kind of rushed into it, and after a few years, it began to crumble, and neither of us had the desire to make it work. She went her way, and I went mine. No hard feelings and no regrets."

He had taken a sip of his coffee, and a big blob of cream was on his nose. Before I mentioned it, I took out my cellphone and snapped a photo.

"I've got cream on my nose? Get it for me," he asked, laughing and handing me the napkin.

I gently wiped the cream from his nose as he looked into my eyes. "You better not share this on Twitter, or I am going to get you good!" he said, laughing.

I didn't have Twitter, but I had Facebook, and I was certainly going to share it. I posted it on my page right then!

"Thank you," he said, smiling. There was a chemistry between us, or it could have been the fact I had needed some love for a long, long time.

"Do you want to go back to my place and chill?" I asked. He was still smiling. "That would be nice," he replied.

I wanted to grab his hand and run up out of there!

But I was cool, calm, and collected. Back at my apartment, my hands were shaking so hard that I had problems getting the keys in the door.

"I hope I'm not making you nervous," he said, moving closer to me.

"No, I'm cool." When we got inside, I invited him to have a seat.

"Do you have any wine?" he asked. Dang, it!

"Let me check."

I did have some wine, so I poured him a glass, and poured myself some ginger ale.

"You don't drink?" he asked.

"No, I don't." I put on some music, sat on the other end of the sofa but not too far away. We talked a little while, and then he moved over closer to me.

"I don't think I'm ready to have sex with anyone yet," I said suddenly.

"Who said anything about having sex?"

"I'm sorry. This is new to me. I don't know what to do. I haven't dated in fitty-leven years. So, you are going to hear some strange things coming out of my mouth," I replied, laughing.

"Just relax. We've already past the hard stuff. I know your name, and you know mine." He put his arm around me, and we just chilled. It was nice; real nice. I was breathing! I didn't even have to remind myself.

29

SINCE I WAS DOING MUCH BETTER, I decided to visit my therapist for a talk. We hadn't seen each other in two years. My life had changed since we'd last spoken, and I wanted to connect with her, only now for different reasons.

Dr. Verlonda was just as glad to see me as I was to see her. We hugged before sitting down across from each other.

"You look great, Benita. So, tell me what's been going on?"
I replied by informing her about my battle with alcoholism and my stint in rehab.
"I'm dating a very nice man, too," I added.
"Oh, really? So, let's start there. Tell me about him."

As I talked about Edgar, I realized midway through the conversation I was falling in love with this man! "Is there a rule book about dating out there? I haven't dated since I was a teenager. I am so confused," I joked.

"Just take it slow and easy. Take as much time as you need to get to know him. Let things flow naturally," she suggested. That was precisely what Edgar had told me on many occasions. I made an appointment to see her in two more weeks.

I took Edgar to meet Daddy over the weekend. We had been seeing each other for nearly six months. I waited because I wanted to make sure we were going to last a while. Trina and my brother, Jimmie, was up from North Carolina. He was teaching high school English and Journalism in Durham.

Daddy and Trina prepared a huge dinner for us. There was food from one end of the table to the other. We all had an enjoyable evening. we got ready to leave, Daddy told Edgar, "Make sure you good care of her and don't hurt her, or you will have to answer to Jimmie and me."

"I promise you, sir. I would never hurt your daughter. I love her." I was taken aback because he had not told me that he loved me.

As we rode back home, Edgar asked, "Would you like to stay the night at my house?"
"Okay," I answered.

30

HE STEPPED IN AND TURNED on the lamp.

"Have a seat; make yourself comfortable. I have to put this food in the fridge," he said. I sat down and waited for him to finish. "Would you like some apple juice?"

"Yes, please," I replied.

He had himself a glass of wine and handed me the apple juice in a wine glass.

"Your dad can throw down in the kitchen! I see where you got your skills," he said, laughing. He removed his shoes, put my legs in his lap, and removed mine. I turned on the television and was about to channel surf when he took the remote from me. "Relax, baby."

"I am relaxed." *One, two, three, four, five, six,*

seven, eight! One, two, three, four, five, six, seven, eight!

Edgar put his arms around me, I never wanted him to take them away. I was feeling him! He took my hand and led me to the bedroom, I nervously followed.

I sat down on the bed while he turned on the radio and went back to the living room to get us something to drink. *One, two, three, four, five, six, seven, eight! One, two, three, four, five, six, seven!*

"Are you nervous?" he asked. I was shaking.

"Yes! I'm nervous!" I took the glass of apple juice from him and gulped it. He chuckled and said again, "Relax."

"Can we dance?" I asked. He looked confused, but he reached out his hand. We stood there, dancing, our bodies firmly pressed together as the music softly played.

Edgar was patient with me, and I appreciated it. I was feeling all kinds of emotions as we lay in each other's arms. The intensity of what we shared was amazing.

"I love you, Benita," he said, looking into my eyes.

I didn't know what to say. I wasn't sure I loved him and I didn't want to say 'thank you'. I smiled and hugged him.

I had only loved one man in my life. What I was feeling right now with Edgar was different than what I had felt from being with Steven. I honestly was not sure what I was feeling, and when I said those words again, I wanted to be sure. It wasn't just that, either. I had been someone's woman since I was seventeen years old; that was thirty years! That was two-thirds of my life. In a couple of months, I would be turning forty-one years old. I wasn't sure if I wanted to be a wife again so soon.

The next morning, I was awakened by Edgar

whispering my name. He had gotten up early and prepared me breakfast in bed. I sat up surprised by his sweetness.

"Let me go freshen up right quick," I said and went to the bathroom.

I squeezed some toothpaste on my finger, swished my mouth out, and splashed some water on my face. Edgar was waiting for me.

He had made French toast, eggs, bacon, fresh fruit, coffee, and juice. I was impressed with his skills in the kitchen.

"I thought your specialty was steaks," I said.
"I have a lot of hidden skills, my lady."
"I see."

He took the tray back into the kitchen. He sat in front of me on the bed and held my hands between his large sweaty ones. "What's going on?" I asked. As soon as I asked it, I knew he was about to ask me to marry him. *One, two, three, four, five!*

"I have something I want to ask you. I'm nervous," Edgar said and laughed. He kissed my hand and reached in his pocket, removing something I could not see.

"I feel like I have been waiting all of my life for someone like you. I never thought I would find it, but God sent you. I am honored, wow! I want to spend the rest of my life with you. Would you do me the honor of being my wife?"

"You know I care about you very much. You are so special to me. I am so flattered that you want me to be your wife; I truly am. Do I have to give you an answer right now?"

"I was hoping you would, but you don't have to. You are saying you want to think about it, right?"

"Yes, I want to think about it. I have spent my entire life trying to find my way to solid ground. And I've just now been able to live with a clear mind and to know myself. I'm not 100 percent yet, though. And you deserve that; I want to be able to give you that. So, yeah. I need time to think about it."

"How much time, baby?"

"I don't know. But I want you to know I do love you. I just want to be able to give you the best of me, and right now, I am not able to do that."

"You are not trying to get rid of me, are you?"

"Boy, no! I love you, Edgar. Can you give me some time?"

"I can do that."

"Thank you, baby," I said and gently kissed him.

I left his apartment that day needing to walk. I had a lot on my mind. He wanted to drive me back home, however, I insisted on walking.

He walked me downstairs and kissed me goodbye again.

"Call me when you get home," he said.

"I promise." I walked up the block, felt the afternoon sun beaming down on me, smelled the fresh vegetables as I passed the bodega on the corner, and heard the music blasting from the radio of an open apartment window.

I felt free and clear for the first time in my life. *One, two, three, four, five, six, seven, eight, nine, ten!* Yeah! I would marry him, but right now, I just wanted to get used to breathing on solid ground.

DARBY WEST

Darby West was born in the Bronx, NY. She moved to Queens when she was a young child. Later on, she moved to rural, Swan Quarter, NC to live with her grandparents. Upon graduating high school, she moved to Brooklyn, New York. She published her first novel, Through the Fire in 2005, followed by The Monkey & the Crocodile, Today I Kissed a Butterfly, and an e-book called Hello Maribeth. Darby currently lives in Winston Salem, NC.